"I wan[   ] to ha[   ]"

Dan stepped forward and put the painting on Cassie's desk. "Cassie." He went on. "When I saw you there, bidding for my painting, I thought—"

"Thought what?" Cassie cut in savagely. "That I was buying it as a sentimental reminder of you? I'll tell you why I wanted it. Yes, it was a reminder. A reminder of the mistake I made loving and believing in a man like you!" She glared at him in disgust. "Did you think if you bought the painting and gave it to me that I'd be grateful, maybe even *very* grateful? Isn't that how it was, Dan? Did I get anything wrong?"

He shook his head. "You couldn't be more wrong. I never intended to hurt you, Cassie, not then ... or now."

MIRANDA LEE was born and brought up in New South Wales, Australia. She had a brief career as cellist in an orchestra, and then another as a computer programmer. A move to the country after marriage and the birth of the first of three daughters limited her career opportunities to being a full-time wife and mother. Encouraged by her family, she began writing in 1982, and acceptance of her first book came after much trial and error. She favors a well-paced, what-happens-next kind of story, but says what matters most "is that my books please and entertain my readers, leaving them feeling good and optimistic about love and marriage in our present topsy-turvy world."

MIRANDA LEE

after the affair

Harlequin Books

TORONTO • NEW YORK • LONDON
AMSTERDAM • PARIS • SYDNEY • HAMBURG
STOCKHOLM • ATHENS • TOKYO • MILAN

Harlequin Presents first edition May 1991
ISBN 0-373-11362-5

Original hardcover edition published in 1990
by Mills & Boon Limited

AFTER THE AFFAIR

CHAPTER ONE

'SOLD! To the lady here in the front row.'

Cassie glanced at the successful buyer sitting next to her, then watched dispiritedly as Lot Forty-Seven was carried away. She sighed. The lovely blue vase would have been a perfect wedding present for her mother and Roger, but seventeen hundred dollars was ridiculously expensive.

'Lot Forty-Eight, ladies and gentlemen. . .a tea-service. . .a fine example of nineteenth-century silver. . .'

Cassie wrinkled her nose and sat back. She didn't like silver. No doubt it was a rare antique, but it was not to her taste.

The bidding started, again without her taking part. Really, the whole auction was proving to be a disappointment. When she'd heard that the river island of Strath-haven had been sold and selected items from the homestead were to be auctioned on site, Cassie had pictured a small affair, with every opportunity of picking up a bargain gift.

Instead, collectors had descended on the property in droves, coming from as far afield as Sydney and Brisbane. Cassie had even noticed a helicopter landing in the grounds when she was arriving.

The prices had been exorbitant, with Cassie growing more and more pessimistic. Her only consolation at the wasted afternoon was that she'd actually been able to visit this place without turning a hair. In nine long years she had avoided even looking at Strath-haven, which wasn't easy, since the island sat in the river directly opposite the Palmer farm.

Admittedly, when she'd driven down to the river and crossed the footbridge that connected the mainland to the island, she had refrained from looking down to the far point and the small building nestling there. But that was only to be expected. She was not a masochist!

The bidding continued, the auctioneer going through another twenty lots with amazing speed. Those Cassie could afford, she didn't like. Those she liked, she couldn't afford.

A glance at her watch told her it was nearly four-thirty. Jason's Saturday afternoon cricket match would be over soon, and if Cassie wasn't home by five her son would badger his grandmother into walking over to the auction. Cassie knew that her mother would be tired after an afternoon keeping the score at cricket, and Cassie already felt guilty over how often her mother looked after Jason, despite the older woman's insistence that she enjoyed it.

'Don't be silly, darling,' her mother had said more than once when Cassie had expressed her concern. 'You are my only child, Jason my only grandchild. I love being with him!'

Nevertheless, Cassie made up her mind to leave the auction after the next few lots.

'And finally, the paintings,' the auctioneer announced. He turned and indicated a selection leaning against the wall behind him. His assistant presented a rather small square-framed canvas, holding it up high before resting it on the table in front of Cassie.

'The first one is Lot Seventy. An untitled, unsigned work by an unknown artist. Yet clearly a work of some merit. And an attractive local landscape, too. Now, ladies and gentlemen, what am I bid. . .?'

Cassie stared.

And stared.

She could hardly believe it.

Her heart began to thud.

She recognised the distinctive use of the pale colours, the broad sweeps of the palette knife, the impressionistic style.

Shocked eyes swept over the scene.

Cassie's stomach churned as she realised that there was only one place where the artist could have set up his easel to paint this picture—where the river was on the left, the suspension bridge in the distance, and the impressive two-storeyed house in which she was now sitting on the right. She had seen that particular view herself many

many times. From the far point of the island, on the riverbank, right next to the small studio.

The studio. . .where Dan had come to stay and paint that fateful summer; where she had posed so innocently for a portrait; where their affair had begun. . .and ended.

A wave of irony washed over Cassie. She thought of all the hours—the *days*—she had spent, wheeling Jason's pram through art galleries in Sydney, searching for one of Dan's paintings. It was a perverse desire. . .wanting to own one, wanting some tangible evidence of his existence. Her mind had kept telling her quite categorically that she should despise the man and never want to see him, or anything belonging to him, again.

Still, she had gone on searching during the entire time it had taken her to complete her veterinary science degree—a foolish, obsessive quest. She had returned home to Riversbend empty-handed, yet this particular painting had been here all along, barely a mile from her home.

'Two thousand. . . Last bid was yours, sir. Any advance on two thousand?'

Cassie came back to the reality of the auction with a jolt. The painting was being sold! Her mouth opened of its own accord. 'Twenty-one hundred.'

Eyes snapped her way. She had not bid before.

Cassie's pulse started racing. She knew that she was doing a mad thing. She was supposed to be buying a present, not giving in to some ghastly sentimental indulgence. It wasn't as though she felt anything for the man any more. Her love for him was well and truly dead. She felt absolutely and positively nothing.

Her heart pounded even faster. Somehow the knowledge that she was acting crazily made no difference. She could not seem to help herself. She wanted that painting!

'Twenty-five!' snapped the man whom she had overbid.

Cassie gritted her teeth. 'Twenty-six.'

There was an electric silence. Cassie held her breath.

'Twenty-seven,' the other bidder gruffed.

Cassie breathed in deeply, trying to calm her growing tension. Should she bid twenty-eight, or leap to three thousand? Which would be the better tactic? Her chest felt as if a vice were squeezing it.

'Three thousand,' she blurted out. And held her breath.

'Thirty-five hundred.'

Disappointment knifed through Cassie, and her chest sagged. She could not go on. She really couldn't. Three thousand had to be her limit.

'It's against you, madam,' the auctioneer said.

She could feel expectant eyes upon her. But she slowly shook her head, her eyes dropping to the floor. She could no longer bear to look at the painting.

'Five thousand dollars!'

A murmur swept through the crowd at the astonishing new bid. Cassie's head snapped round. She knew that voice! Her eyes clawed through the sea of faces. It couldn't be him. It *couldn't*. . .

There was no reason why he should be here. No reason at all. . .

And then she saw him, standing near one of the back windows, looking as devastating as ever.

Dan McKay.

His black eyes locked fiercely on to hers, and a stab of pure pain sliced through Cassie. She jerked her head round to face the front, shaken to the core of her being.

'Going once, twice. . . Sold!'

Cassie jumped when the gavel banged down. Then she sat. At first frozen, then suddenly trembling. If someone had asked her before this moment what was left of her feelings for Dan McKay she would have said nothing. *Nothing*! She would have sworn that he could not move a single emotion in her.

But she had been wrong. Something dark and destructive, something unexpected and shocking, had stirred inside her. It spun her head back to seek him out again.

He was moving towards the front of the room,

his gaze never leaving hers. But his eyes were guarded, making it impossible to tell what he was thinking. Cassie's mouth grew dry as she watched him approach. He was so handsome still, each line of his strong, angular face and tall, lean body achingly familiar.

Yet there were differences, Cassie conceded ruefully. The unruly black waves of nine years ago had been cut short and, while the well-groomed style complemented his dark suit and white shirt, he was a far cry from the informal, bejeaned Dan whom Cassie had once known. This man was smooth and suave and sophisticated, the epitome of city elegance.

Dan was watching her as well, waiting perhaps for a visible reaction to his shock return. When she gave none, sitting silent and staring, he smiled, his straight black eyebrows lifting enquiringly.

Again it sliced through her, sharper now and more definite, tightening her stomach, setting her teeth hard in her jaw. Hatred! Pure and utter hatred!

The feeling was so shockingly intense that she must have projected it in her eyes, for the smile was instantly wiped from his face, his expression changing to one of puzzlement.

A wave of fierce resentment swept through Cassie at his lack of sensitivity. Who did he think he was, coming back here, smiling at her as if everything had been forgiven and forgotten? Nothing was forgiven! Nothing was forgotten!

No doubt his return had something to do with buying back his painting. Nothing else would have brought him back, she decided cynically. And no doubt he would be gone again at the end of the auction.

Meanwhile. . .

Cassie gritted her teeth and looked up. He was talking to the auctioneer's assistant, yet glancing impatiently her way. A jolt of sudden panic set her heart racing. Jason! Oh, God, she had forgotten about Jason!

Her mind whirled. It was imperative that Dan didn't accidentally find out about the boy during his visit. Imperative! Instinct told Cassie that Dan was not a man who would ignore a son, even if the mother meant nothing to him any longer.

Cassie knew that she had to get out of this room, away from him. To meet him and talk to him—however briefly—was a risk she wasn't prepared to take.

She should have left without looking back. She should have just stood up and walked away. But something—female curiosity, perhaps—drew her to one final glance.

It was a mistake. He was staring at her over the man's shoulder, and when their eyes met he held hers easily. They had always been her undoing. His eyes. They were like molten ebony, their deep-set, penetrating scrutiny searing its way into her soul, evoking long-buried memories from deep inside.

She tried to look away, but could not.

She was transfixed, hypnotised. Her heart began to pound and, as his gaze went deeper and deeper, Cassie's mind plunged her back. . .back. . .till she was lying on the rug on the studio floor, gazing passionately up at him. He was standing over her, proud and virile, his eyes devouring her, arousing her, teasing her, till she could bear it no longer. She held her arms out to him, and as he knelt down she reached out, gathering his naked body to hers with a sighing, tormented groan.

Cassie jerked back to the present, a cold sweat breaking out on her forehead. She wrenched her eyes away from his and jumped up, clusmy in her haste, but intent only on one purpose. To flee.

CHAPTER TWO

Dan caught her on the veranda.

'Cassie?' His hand closed over a wrist, spinning her to a halt.

Terrified eyes lifted to him.

'You're not leaving, are you?' He peered down at her with that inscrutable black gaze of his.

Cassie tried desperately to pull herself together. You are twenty-nine years old, she reassured herself. You are a competent veterinary surgeon. You are an independent, clear-thinking woman. You are *not* a vulnerable, naïve girl barely out of her teens.

She dragged in a steadying breath and schooled her face into a bland smile. 'Hello, Dan,' she said. 'I thought it was you in there. It's been a long time. You're looking well. Sorry, but I can't stay and chat. I'm running late.'

His hand remained closed around her wrist, effectively staying her. 'Then you didn't leave the auction because of me?' His eyes were searching hers, trying no doubt to gauge her reaction to him.

The intensity of his expression unnerved and annoyed Cassie. Who did he think he was, giving

her the third degree after running into her out of
sheer coincidence? He couldn't possibly have
known that she would attend this auction.

Her laugh carried the right amount of dry
disdain. 'Good heavens, no. Why should I do
that?'

He frowned. Clearly her attitude puzzled him.
The reason why eluded Cassie. 'Then could you
spare me a few minutes?' he asked, still frowning.
'I won't keep you long.'

She glanced at her watch, then up. 'Perhaps a
minute, then.' Her voice held an impatient note.

'So kind,' he muttered, and dropped her wrist.

Cassie tried not to let her relief show. It was
unbearable having him touch her. Unbearable!

'You'll have to make it snappy, Dan. I really
must be going.'

His head tilted slightly to one side, eyes narrowing. His gaze flicked down over her body, clad
casually in faded blue jeans and a pink cotton
shirt. When he looked back up at her face, his
expression thoughtful, Cassie found herself wishing she'd had time to change before coming to the
auction. But she'd been running late after an
emergency at the surgery, and had had only a
minute to dash on some pink lipstick and flick a
quick brush through her fine blonde hair.

At that moment she wanted more than anything
to be able to present an image as cool and
sophisticated as Dan's. The feeling that she was at

a physical disadvantage was as annoying as his close scrutiny.

'You know, you've hardly changed,' he said slowly. 'You're still incredibly beautiful. . .still without artifice.'

Her cheeks burnt with hot resentment. Her jaw clenched in anger. Trust him to resort to flattery. What a hide he had! And what a fool she was to let him still affect her, even if it was just irritation now. But two could play that game.

'You're hardly the worse for wear, either,' she countered in an offhand tone.

His mouth lifted in a dry smile. 'You flatter me. I'll be forty next year, and I feel every day of it.'

Cassie was taken aback. She hadn't realised he was that old. Nine years ago he had looked as if he were in his middle twenties, no more. But it didn't change anything. In fact, it made his guilt even worse. He should have known better than to toy with a young girl's life.

She waited for him to say something further, but he didn't. He had always been a man of few words.

'What is it you want, then?' she snapped irritably.

He drew back a step and flourished his hand in the direction of the front doors. 'If you will accompany me inside, I'll show you.'

'What do you mean. . .inside? I'm not going back into the auction. I told you. I have to go.'

'I know what you told me. . .' His determined glance indicated that he'd totally ignored all she had said. 'We'll go into the library. It's the first door on the right.'

'We can't do that!'

'Why not?'

'The owner might not like it.'

'He won't mind.'

Her eyes grew wary. 'How do you know that? Do you know him?'

'Very well.'

Cassie tried to control her growing alarm. She'd heard that the new owner of Strath-haven was a wealthy businessman from Sydney, intent on using the island as a rural retreat, in much the same way as the van Aarks had done. If Dan was a friend of his, as he had been of the van Aarks, perhaps he would be staying here as a guest sometimes. Oh, God. . .

'Stop frowning, Cassie,' he advised. 'It spoils your lovely forehead.'

She threw him a scornful look. 'I'll come inside, but please. . .stop the flattery. Keep that for your current victims. It won't work on me any more.'

He stiffened at her barb, but she gained no satisfaction from it. Strange, she puzzled, that she didn't enjoy hurting him. Surely he deserved it? Surely he deserved anything she could dish out?

'Come along,' he ground out, taking her elbow in a firm grip.

When she instinctively pulled back, he sighed and lessened the force of his hold. But he still urged her towards the front doors. Cassie went, not knowing what else to do. He wasn't going to take no for an answer, that was obvious. And she knew that she should find out what the situation was—if he was going to be around on a regular basis.

A churning thought had come to her. Perhaps he worked for the new owner of Strath-haven. After all, artists rarely made enough to live on.

Going with him proved to be a mistake. She had underestimated the physical effect he still had on her. His fingers felt like silken threads on the soft flesh of her inner arm, sending warm shivers through her veins, and when he stopped to open the library door the still reality of his closeness became particularly disturbing. All she had to do was turn and she would be in his arms. All she had to do was signal her willingness and he would sweep her into the room, shut the door and kiss her.

She knew that this was so, for Dan McKay was that sort of man. The type who would take a woman quite ruthlessly—if she showed weakness—all the while pretending she was someone special, then discard her if and when it was expedient.

'This won't take long, will it?' she asked sharply, and took a step backwards. She was worried that he might grow aware of her quickened heartbeat, her flush of sexual awareness.

He pushed the door open, then glared down at her. Light from the room slanted brilliantly across his face and Cassie was shocked to see that he *had* aged, though he still didn't look anywhere near forty. A smattering of grey was hiding within the thick black waves and there were lines around his dark eyes.

But neither detracted from his appeal. If anything, they added a dimension of rugged sophistication to his looks that he had perhaps lacked all those years ago. Or perhaps it appealed to her now because she herself was older.

'If you'd stop backing away from me,' he said curtly, 'we'd be a damned sight quicker!'

Cassie tipped up her chin and strode past him, dropping her holdall in a distant chair before whirling round to face him.

He was watching her closely 'Far enough away for you?' he mocked. 'Shall I keep the door open as well?'

She said nothing. But her stomach muscles tightened as he swung the door shut. An impatient sigh betrayed his frustration.

'I won't hold you up now,' he said brusquely, moving to pick up the painting, which she hadn't noticed lying on top of a large desk, 'but I wanted you to have this.'

Cassie's mouth dropped open. Confusion and

anger warred with an irrational pleasure. 'But why?' she blurted out before recovering. 'I . . . No, thank you. I don't want it. I won't take it!'

His face was annoyingly passive. 'Why not? You were bidding for it.'

She gulped down a gathering lump of panic. 'That doesn't mean I'll take it from you.'

'Why not?'

His persistence brought an agitated mutter. 'This is ridiculous!'

'Is there someone who would object to your taking a gift from me? A lover, perhaps?'

She glared at him. 'I don't have to answer your questions, Dan McKay!'

'No, you don't,' he said with maddening composure.

There was a short, sharp silence.

'I could well have a husband by now, for all you know,' she threw at him.

'But you don't, do you?'

She gasped. 'How do you know that? Have you been spying on me?'

She saw the surprise on his face and knew that she was over-reacting badly.

He walked over and picked up her hand. Her stomach somersaulted as his long, elegant fingers stroked her palm, her fingers. 'You're not wearing a ring,' he explained.

She snatched her hand away, but not before her

breathing had gone absolutely haywire. 'I might have taken it off,' she argued breathlessly.

'And have you?' His black eyes were watchful.

She lifted her chin. 'No.'

'So there's no husband. What about lovers? Any of those around at the moment?'

Her blue eyes flashed angrily at his hounding of her private life. 'My having or not having a lover is none of your business.'

'I'm making it my business.'

She was shocked by the implication of his statement. 'My God!' she exclaimed. 'Do you honestly think you can come back here after all these years and take up where you left off?'

His eyes were giving her no peace. They were devouring her, yet telling her nothing.

'I didn't think anything, Cassie,' he said matter-of-factly. 'But when I saw you in there, bidding for my painting, I thought——'

'Thought what?' she cut in savagely. 'That I was buying it as a sentimental reminder of you?' She laughed—a harsh, cynical sound. 'You do have a colossal ego, don't you? I'll tell you why I wanted that painting of yours. Yes, it was as a reminder. A reminder of the mistake I made in loving and believing in a man like you! But now I don't need it, do I? I've seen you again, experienced at first hand another sample of your amazing sense of opportunity.' She glared at him in disgust. 'I can just imagine what you felt in there when you saw me bidding for your painting. An initial surprise, perhaps, but quickly followed by a smug satisfaction. An old flame, you would have thought, who hasn't forgotten the good times we once shared. She even wants my painting as a memento. What good luck! I wonder what would happen if I bought the painting and made a grand gesture of giving it to her. She would be bound to be grateful, maybe even *very* grateful. . .'

Cassie stopped, and let a mask of stone drop over her heated features. 'Isn't that how it was, Dan? Did I get anything wrong?'

He was staring at her with such a look of horror that for a moment Cassie wondered if she could indeed be wrong.

He shook his head. 'You couldn't be more wrong. I never intended to hurt you, Cassie. Not then. . .or now.'

His rich voice reverberated with such apparent sincerity that Cassie almost weakened. But she didn't. For this was Dan McKay speaking, she reminded herself coldly. Accomplished artist, lover, liar and adulterer!

'Hurt me?' she tossed off airily. 'Don't lose any sleep on my account. I'm well and truly over you now, believe me.'

He frowned at her, but said nothing. Cassie hated his silence. She remembered how when she'd posed for him hours had gone by without his saying a word. She had chattered away, telling him everything about herself, but he'd never reciprocated. It wasn't until he'd left her that she'd known why.

'What are you doing here, anyway?' she demanded. 'Riversbend is a long way from the bright lights of Sydney.'

When her tart words brought an assessing look from Dan, Cassie regretted asking. She hoped he wouldn't think she was interested in him, despite her outburst.

'A change is as good as a rest,' he said cryptically.

A prickle of apprehension darted up Cassie's spine. 'Oh?'

'I needed some fresh air.' He walked over to stare through the large window at the river below. 'I've always loved this place. When I found out it was on the market. . .'

Cassie's heart stopped. Surely he couldn't mean. . .?

He turned slowly, saw her widening eyes. 'I decided to buy it. Yes, Cassie, I'm the new owner of Strath-haven.'

CHAPTER THREE

CASSIE went weak at the knees.

'I'll be your next-door neighbour,' Dan added, his hands slipping into his trouser pockets. 'That is. . .if you still live on the farm across the river.'

She didn't know what to say. The feeling of impending doom was overwhelming. It was all she could do to keep standing.

'I gather that idea doesn't find favour,' Dan said drily.

Cassie stared at him. 'You really o-own Strathhaven?' she stammered.

'You sound doubtful.'

'But how?' she blurted out. 'I mean. . .'

He gave her a sharp look. 'I've done well enough over the years.'

'But. . .but you're an artist. I was told that the new owner was a businessman!'

'Can't I be both?' His face softened for a moment. 'Look, Cassie, I'm not an artist by profession. Painting's a hobby of mine. . .a pastime.'

His admission swept all thought of Jason aside for the moment. All Cassie could think of was how little she'd known about Dan at the time of their affair, how little he had told her! It hurt terribly to be reminded of her foolish naïveté.

'Do forgive my stupidity,' she said tartly. 'A pastime. . . How quaint! Just as your models were pastimes?'

His sigh carried frustration. 'You know that's not true. And I never said I made my living as an artist.'

'You never said much at all, Dan,' she accused.

Silence descended. They looked at each other for several seconds, Cassie with bitter resentment, Dan with an undermining concern.

'Why are you so hostile, Cassie? After all this time.'

'Hostile, Dan? I'm not hostile. I'm merely saying a few of the things I never had the opportunity to say nine years ago. You did leave rather quickly.' Her glare held shivers of ice. 'But that's all water under the bridge, isn't it? The present is far more to the point. I gather you won't be living here permanently? This will be a weekender, or some such?'

Already she was devising a plan to protect herself and her son. Her mother and Roger were getting married soon. They could have the house across the river. She could move, to Roger's place in town maybe, or to another town altogether!

'I shall be travelling back and forth to Sydney,' he admitted slowly, 'but I *had* intended spending as much time here as I could.'

Her mind jumped on the way he'd said 'had intended'. She clutched at the straw. 'And you've changed your mind?'

'That depends.'

'On what?'

He shrugged. 'On a lot of things.' He gave her the oddest look. It was vaguely challenging. 'Meanwhile. . .don't you think we could at least be friends? After all, we will be neighbours. How about coming back when this auction is over? Have dinner with me this evening. You could advise me on what to buy for the house. I did keep the essentials in furniture, but the rest will need a woman's touch.'

Cassie stared at him in utter astonishment. 'You don't give up easily, do you?'

'No.'

'I can't,' she said sharply. 'Sorry.'

'Can't or won't?'

'Both!'

'Why not?'

Cassie's head was whirling. Why not? God, if only he knew. . .

But he would know, she thought frantically, if he meant to really live here. Even if she moved, some day, someone would say something about Jason. And Dan would come looking for him.

Fear made her aggressive. 'I think your wife is a good reason for me not to come, don't you?'

There was no doubting his shock, but he

recovered quickly. 'I see. . . So that's it. You found out.'

'The van Aarks were only too pleased to enlighten me.'

'And what exactly did they tell you?' he said angrily, and paced towards her. 'For pity's sake, Cassie, they didn't even know the whole truth.' His hands closed over her shoulders. 'They weren't close friends, just social acquaintances. God! Do you think I confided my private affairs to people like them?'

Cassie was crazily aware of the bruising fingers digging into her shoulders. Her breathing grew fast and shallow. Her face flushed. 'Let me go!' she gasped in a panic.

'No!' he snarled. 'Not till you've listened to the truth. I was separated from my wife when I came here to stay at the island. We were getting a divorce. I didn't mean to fall in love with you, dammit! But you were so lovely. . . so goddamned lovely. I convinced myself that I'd be content with painting you, being with you, listening to you give voice to your bright, sweet dreams for the future. What a fool I was to think that I wouldn't end up making love to you! But I did *love* you, Cassie, and I meant to marry you at the time. You have to believe that!'

Believe him? He expected her to believe him? *Believing* in Dan had been her greatest mistake.

She wrenched out of his hold with a violent

twist. 'Save your breath, Dan,' she said savagely. 'You're wasting it on me.'

He visibly fought anger at her rejection of his plea.

'Something wrong, Dan?' she mocked. 'Your plans going awry?'

New resolve firmed his face. 'Cassie, I understand how bad it must have looked. I really do. And I can see how hurt you've been, but you must listen. My wife had an accident—a terrible accident. She——'

'I know about the accident,' she interrupted bluntly. 'The van Aarks told me that, too. But *you* didn't, Dan, when you sent me my "Dear John" letter. No mention of any accident. No mention of any wife. Shall I tell you what you said? Shall I remind you?'

His mouth clamped shut in thinly disguised frustration.

'"Dear Cassie,"' she went on in sharp, bitter tones. '"I hate having to write to you like this. I would much rather be able to see you personally. To explain. But it is best that I stay right away. You are young. You will forget me in time. And, I hope, forgive me. I want you to get on with your life, my darling girl. Be a wonderful veterinary surgeon, make some man a wonderful wife, some child a wonderful mother. My love always. Dan."'

She glared at him when she had finished, head

held high, eyes smarting with the salt of unshed tears.

He looked appalled. 'You know it. . .off by heart?'

She turned away from his sight, unwilling to have him witness her distress. She heard him approach, felt his warm breath on the back of her neck. Her heart stopped when his hands closed gently over her shoulders.

'Oh, Cassie, Cassie,' he murmured in her hair. 'I didn't tell you about my wife in the letter because I thought it would only add to your hurt. She needed me in a way I didn't think I could adequately explain. It was far too complex.'

'But *I* needed you, Dan,' Cassie choked out, forgetting everything but the way he was enfolding her back against his chest, forgetting every. . .single. . .thing.

'I know. . .I know. . .' He was holding her tightly, his lips against her ear. 'But you were young and strong, my darling. You could cope. . . I had no option then. But I'm back now. Can't you see? I'm back. . .'

He turned her slowly, tilted up her chin. She caught her breath as his mouth descended.

His kiss was soft and tender. . .sweet. His thumb was tracing her jawline, a finger stroking the sensitive flesh of her throat.

Subtly, slowly, his mouth grew more insistent, his tongue probing at her hypnotised lips. They parted slightly, allowing him entry, then further and further. Fire ignited along her veins, and before she knew it she was kissing him back with all the fervour of passions that had been buried for nine lonely years. This was the man she had once loved. This was the man who——

'My God!'

She wrenched herself out of his arms, shocked and shaking.

'My God!' she repeated, chest heaving, eyes awash.

'Cassie, I. . .' He reached for her.

'Don't!' she sobbed. 'Don't touch me! Don't say a word.'

He didn't do either. But he was clearly upset.

And why wouldn't he be? Cassie thought with bitter fury as she struggled to get control of herself. For a moment there he must have thought he'd struck the jackpot! Only back at Riversbend for an hour and, with a few half-truths smoothly delivered, he already had a willing bedmate in his clutches.

The glaring facts catapulted into her brain. He'd run into her by sheer coincidence at the auction. He certainly hadn't come back for *her*. He hadn't even known till he'd seen her hand whether she was married or not. In nine years she could very well have moved away somewhere. Or died! And as for that pathetic excuse about his wife not being able to cope. . .

Oh, God! His wife! And what about children? Had the marriage produced children? She hated the very thought, but she had to find out.

Her eyes slashed at him. 'What about your wife? Your children?' she demanded, heart racing.

'I have no children,' came the brusque reply.

Cassie swallowed. 'And your wife? Where's she? Will she be living here with you?'

'No.'

'Another convenient separation?'

'No.'

'What, then?'

His face was grim. 'My wife. . .is dead.'

Cassie was rocked, as much by the announcement as by an unwanted sympathy for Dan. He sounded so. . .desolate.

'When?' she rasped.

'Just over a year ago.'

Any sympathy vanished. 'A year ago,' she repeated flatly. Twelve whole months. Fifty-two weeks. Three hundred and sixty-five days. More than enough time to contact her. . . If he truly cared. It was the final nail in his coffin. 'I see,' she said in a flat, lifeless voice.

'You don't see at all!' Dan growled. 'You've taken everything the wrong way. You don't believe I still care about you!'

'No,' she stated with cruel honesty. 'I don't.'

'Hell!' He raked his hands through his hair,

disturbing the veneer of polished elegance. The dishevelled waves reminded her of the Dan she had first met—the slightly messy, struggling artist. Or so she had believed at the time.

But it had all been an act, a game, a fantasy.

Cassie turned away. She didn't want to be reminded of the past. She had been such a little fool then. She had no intention of being one again.

Suddenly, she remembered and looked at her watch. After five. . . If she wasn't home soon her mother would be sure to come looking for her.

'I have to go,' she said brusquely, and moved towards the door.

Dan was there before her. He opened it, but barred her exit. 'No. Let's get it all straight between us, Cassie. There's too much that's been left unexplained.'

Her eyes were hard. 'You're too late, Dan. Get out of my way.'

He glared at her for a moment, then stepped aside. 'I won't let it finish like this, Cassie,' he said as she walked past him. 'You must know that.'

She stopped and eyed him fiercely over her shoulder. 'And you must know, Dan, that I'm a grown woman now. I have a mind of my own. No one, least of all you, forces me to do anything!'

She set her jaw, suddenly determined to act out her strong words. She would not run away. She would not move. If and when Dan found out about Jason, she would deal with it. He might not discover the boy's existence for ages. He might even quit Strath-haven before doing so.

Dan was watching her with a reproachful expression. 'You've grown hard, Cassie.'

'No, Dan, just wise. . .wise to men like you.'

'I'm not what you think.'

Her smile was cold. 'Goodbye, Dan. Live here if you must, but don't cross that bridge. Don't try to see me.'

'And if I do?'

She swept on, away from his veiled threat, away from her treacherous responses. She should never have let him kiss her. Never! But, oh. . .the pleasure his lips evoked, the desire his touch uncurled.

She stuffed a fist in her mouth to stifle her moan of dismay and hurried on, down the hall, past the noisy auction-room, out into the bright, bright sunshine, there to grind to a horrified halt.

Her mother was coming across the suspension bridge. And running ahead, up the hill, through the hedge, his legs going like pistons, his hair flying, was Jason.

A noise behind her had Cassie whirling.

It was Dan, holding her denim bag. 'You forgot this,' he said.

Stricken, she didn't know where to turn, where to look.

'Mum! Mum!' Jason called as he raced up the stairs to meet her.

CHAPTER FOUR

CASSIE heard Dan's sharp intake of breath. When he stepped forward to be level with her, a swift glance verified his utter shock.

Her eyes flew back to her son, travelling anxiously over his slight figure as he bounced up on to the veranda. Jason was not overly big for his age, so there was some hope that Dan would not put two and two together.

But it was a slim hope. She only had to look frankly at the boy to know that Dan wouldn't be fooled for long. He might not be an artist by profession, but he had an artist's keen observation, and while Jason's hair was mid-brown and quite straight, not at all like Dan's thick black waves, the eyes were a dead giveaway. They were jet black, deep-set and piercing. The exact image of his father's.

Jason reached the veranda, coming to an untidy halt in front of her. 'We won, Mum. We won! Isn't that terrific? And guess what—next week I'm going to have a go as wicket-keeper.'

She dared not look Dan's way, but she could feel the electric tension emanating from his rock-like body. 'That's wonderful, love,' she said, and gave Jason a hug. Be damned with you, Dan McKay! she thought defiantly.

'Hey, Mum, did you see that helicopter over there? Isn't it terrific? Wouldn't I just love to have a ride in that!'

Cassie grimaced at her son's prattle. All she wanted to do was get away. The situation was excruciating for her. She was afraid that the penny would drop and Dan would make a scene. 'Jason, I don't think——'

'That could be arranged,' Dan interrupted curtly, 'since it's my helicopter to do with as I wish.'

Cassie whirled to face him. '*Yours*?' She was still unable to take in Dan's unexpected wealth.

'Mine!' He gave her a hard, penetrating look before returning his attention to Jason, a grim concentration drawing his dark eyebrows together.

'Oh, boy! Did you hear that, Mum?'

She gave a weak nod.

Jason glanced from his mother to Dan. 'Are you a friend of Mum's, mister?'

The corner of Dan's mouth twisted. 'I was. . .a long time ago.'

'And you really own that helicopter?'

Dan flicked a caustic glance Cassie's way. 'I seem to be having trouble making people believe anything I say. Yes, Jason, it is indisputably my helicopter.'

'Wow! Can I have a ride in it today? Now?'

'If you like.'

'Jason, I don't——'

'A ride in a helicopter!' Jason exclaimed, not even hearing his mother's objection. His beaming face was turned towards the helicopter. 'Oh, boy! Wait till Gran hears about this!'

Cassie groaned.

The sound drew a puzzled glance from her son. 'Are you all right, Mum? You look kinda sick, or something.'

'I. . .I have a headache. I'm afraid you'll have to leave Mr McKay's offer of a ride for today.'

'Aw, gee. . .'

Dan knelt down to Jason's eye level. 'Not to worry,' he said kindly. 'There'll be plenty of other days. By the way, how old are you, Jason?'

Cassie's heart stopped.

'Eight,' her son announced proudly, then added, 'I'll be nine in November.'

'Nine, eh?' Dan lifted his dark eyes to glare daggers at Cassie. 'In November, no less. . .'

It took all her inner strength to glare proudly back at him.

So now he knew for certain! It had been inevitable that he would. But what was he going to do about it? Cassie was so upset by the possibilities that her head was indeed pounding.

Dan straightened up, just as Cassie's mother

puffed up the steep steps. 'My goodness, but that's a walk! Jason, you shouldn't tear ahead like that.'

Mrs Palmer's arrival did nothing to alleviate Cassie's distress. Her mother wouldn't recognise Dan, as they had never actually met, but she would know his name. Cassie hoped and prayed that she would be able to escape without effecting an introduction, but, knowing her mother, that was unlikely.

Joan Palmer was still a good-looking woman at fifty-five, with stylishly cut grey-blonde hair and a shapely figure. People said that Cassie was the spitting image of her mother as a young girl, but where Cassie was a modern, independent woman, her mother was one of the old school, who believed that the female sex was put on earth solely for the purpose of marriage. She would not miss a chance of meeting a handsome man, especially one whom she might be able to push in her daughter's direction.

Cassie's anti-social behaviour had been a source of several heated discussions over the years. The 'once bitten, twice shy' principle did not go down well at all, though Cassie could have pointed out that it had taken her mother almost nine years herself to get over her own husband's death. Roger Nolan, Cassie's employer, had been wanting to marry the attractive widow Palmer for years, but Joan had only recently given him the nod. The wedding was due to take place in two weeks' time.

Perhaps finally aware that she was staring at Dan, Joan swung her attention to her daughter. 'Well, love? Did you have any luck at the auction?'

'I'm afraid not, Mum. Everything was much too dear.'

'Guess what, Gran,' Jason piped in. 'This man here's an old friend of Mum's and he owns that helicopter over there and he's going to give me a ride in it some time, aren't you, mister?'

'I guarantee it.'

'See? He——'

'Hush, Jason.' Joan smiled apologetically at Dan. 'That's very kind of you, Mr. . .er. . . Cassie, aren't you going to introduce us?'

Cassie steeled herself. It wasn't going to be easy introducing a mother to the man who'd made her unmarried daughter pregnant. And Joan was bound to recognise the name at once.

Cassie's sigh carried a weary resignation. 'Mum, this is the new owner of Strath-haven, Mr McKay. . .Mr *Dan McKay*.'

'Pleased to meet you, Mr Mc. . . Oh. . .' Her ready smile faded, her outstretched hand dropped. 'Oh, dear. . .'

It was a dreadful moment, saved by a child's innocence.

'Pleased to meet you, Mr McKay.' Jason's hand shot out like a fast ball at cricket.

'You can call me Dan, Jason.'

Cassie stiffened. It had sounded like 'Dad'. 'I think Jason should——'

'Dan will be fine,' he overrode her firmly. 'I prefer it.'

'Are you really going to be living here, Dan?' Jason asked, black eyes shining with uninhibited joy.

'I certainly am.'

'Oh, boy! Can I come over and visit sometimes? I won't be a bother. Really I won't.'

'Any time. . .son.'

The word sent a stab of fear into Cassie. She looked at Dan appealingly. Please, don't tell him, her eyes said. Please. . .

His returning look was so cold, it sent shivers up her spine.

'Did you hear that, Mum?'

'Yes, Jason, I heard,' Cassie choked out. 'Now we really must be going. Nice to have seen you again, Dan,' she added stiffly and took her bag from him. 'Are you coming, Mum?'

Joan looked as if she'd been struck by lightning. 'Oh. . . Yes. . . Of course. . . Goodbye, Mr. . . er. . . Goodbye. . .'

Cassie took her mother's arm and helped her down the steps, not once looking back over her shoulder. Jason, as was his habit, skipped on ahead, shouting, 'Oh, boy! Oh, boy!' in a happy, excited voice.

Cassie kept a firm grip on herself as she walked away. But it wasn't easy. She was tempted to turn round, to run back, to beg Dan not to spoil what she had built up for herself and her son over the last nine years. He had no right, no right at all to come back into her life now and turn it upside-down again. She didn't need him. *Jason* didn't need him. Her son had never suffered from not having a father. And he would gain little from acquiring one now. Particularly one not married to his mother. Riversbend would be agog!

'Cassie. . .'

'What?' she snapped, her angry thoughts having fuelled a short fuse. 'Sorry, Mum,' she added quickly. 'I'm still a bit. . .upset.'

'I don't blame you, love. It must have come as a big shock, seeing Dan McKay again, finding out he'd bought Strath-haven. Then having Jason burst in on you like he did.'

Cassie sighed. They were about to step on to the suspension bridge. Jason was up ahead in the centre, jumping up and down, enjoying the effect he was having. Not so his mother.

'Jason! For Pete's sake, stand still or move along. Do you want your Gran and myself to end up in the river?'

He looked up, not at all chastened. 'Sorry, Mum,' he shouted back, and ran on, which wasn't much of an improvement on using the bridge as a trampoline. It swooped and swayed under their feet.

'That boy!' Cassie complained.

'Perhaps he needs a father's hand,' her mother said softly.

Cassie's glance was sharp. 'And what do you mean by that?'

Her mother gave her one of those innocent 'Are you talking to me?' looks. 'Nothing. . . Nothing.'

'Oh, yes, you did! You think that just because Dan's handsome and rich I should try to get him to marry me, don't you?'

Joan shrugged. 'Well, he doesn't exactly fit the mental picture I've had of him over the years. I imagined him as a shaggy-haired painting bum, with a three-day growth on his chin and not a cent to his name. Let's face it, Cassie, the Dan McKay I saw this afternoon has a lot going for him.'

'Oh, Mum! So Dan's successful and spruced up now. So what? That's all surface gloss. Don't be taken in by it. And give me credit for some pride. You know how deeply he hurt me!'

'Yes, Cassie, I do, but that was a long time ago, love. People make mistakes and life goes on. Perhaps you——' She broke off and stopped abruptly. The bridge shuddered. 'Oh, dear. . . I just realised. . . I. . .I'd forgotten he was married.'

'His wife died a while back,' Cassie announced

bluntly. 'Not that that makes any difference. And before you ask. . .no, he hasn't any other children.'

'Gran! Mum! Come on!'

'Coming, Jason,' Cassie called, and they walked on in agitated silence.

'What do you think he's going to do about Jason?' Joan said at last. 'I mean. . .it's quite obvious that he guessed. And who wouldn't? Why didn't you ever tell me about the eyes? There I was thinking they were a throwback to old Uncle Bart.'

'Do we have to keep talking about this, Mum?' Cassie said impatiently. 'I'd like to forget it.'

'It's a bit hard to forget the man when he's going to be living next door.'

'This isn't the city,' Cassie argued hotly. 'It's not as though we're at leaning-over-the-fence distance from each other. He's a good mile away.'

'Don't be ridiculous, Cassie. You know full well he isn't going to forget *you*. Or Jason. I saw the way he was looking at the boy. Hungry, that man. Hungry for love. . .'

Cassie felt a sick pang in the pit of her stomach. There were many types of hunger, she wanted to say to her mother. And it certainly wasn't love on Dan's mind. Possession might be closer to the mark.

'I might let him see Jason occasionally, but he

needn't think he's going to tell all and sundry he's my son's father,' she said indignantly.

Her mother gave a dry laugh. 'And who's to stop him? Something tells me Dan McKay is not an easy man to handle. Once he's set his mind on something. . .'

Joan's words reminded Cassie of what Dan had said at the library door. . . 'I won't let it finish like this, Cassie.'

And that had been *before* he'd found out about his son! It was all too much for Cassie.

'Here, Mum,' she said, handing her mother the keys as they reached the other side of the river. 'You take the jeep and drive on up home with Jason. I want to see to the horses before it gets dark.'

'You and those horses!'

'I won't be long,' Cassie called as she walked away along the riverbank.

She dimly heard her mother grumble something about dying of starvation, but she kept walking. Actually, the horses didn't need attention. They'd been looked over, fed and watered that morning, but she desperately needed a few quiet moments away from her mother's probing, away from Jason's high-spirited chatter. And she needed time: time to soothe her chaotic nerves, time to think.

All the horses pricked up their ears at her coming, but only Rosie whinnied and trotted to

the fence for a pat. The mare's unconditional
affection tugged at Cassie's heart. If only people
were like that.

Rosie had been eighteen years old, barren and
in a deplorable condition when Cassie had saved
her from the knacker's yard. People who saw her
now could not believe she was the same be-
draggled animal of eighteen months before. Not
only was she blooming with health, but a foal was
on the way.

'Hello, old thing,' Cassie said, running knowl-
edgeable eyes over the mare's rump. There were
no tell-tale hollows near the tail. 'No foal tonight,
I see. That's good. You have to keep carrying that
baby for another month, Rosie, so stick with it,
my girl.'

Rosie nodded her head up and down as if in
agreement.

Cassie sighed and curled an arm around the
horse's neck. 'The man who gave me my baby has
come back, Rosie. You don't know Dan. He was
before your time. But I don't love him any more.
In fact, I hate him! But that's not the problem. Or
maybe it is. You see. . .'

She leant closer and pressed her cheek up
against the warmth of the horse's mane. 'I have
this ghastly confession to make,' Cassie whispered
huskily. 'I detest myself for it, but. . .the truth
is. . .when Dan kissed me in the library, for a
moment I didn't want him to stop. After all this

time. . .it felt the same. And how can that be? How can it, when I hate him so?'

As though sensing Cassie's distress, Rosie hung over the fence and nuzzled her mistress's hand. I'm here, the gesture seemed to say. Everything will be all right.

Cassie sighed and straightened. She gave the mare a farewell stroke then turned for the long walk home.

Half-way up the hill Cassie stopped and glanced over her shoulder. A lone figure was standing on the veranda of Strath-haven, and, though it was indiscernible from that distance and in the fading light, Cassie knew that it was Dan.

A shiver ran up her spine. He was watching her. Watching her and already planning his next move.

For, despite her warning him not to, Cassie knew that he *would* cross the river. He would come, if not for her then for his son. It was as inevitable as the sun setting that evening and rising the next morning.

The only question was. . .how soon?

CHAPTER FIVE

ROGER turned from the dining-room window, a glass of port in his hand. 'I hear your new neighbour is quite a man,' he directed at Cassie.

She glanced up from the table to look squarely at her boss. Though almost sixty years old, Roger was still dapper, with short grey hair, a neat moustache and an insatiable curiosity about people.

It was this last facet of his character that had Joan frowning madly at her daughter. Roger knew nothing of the circumstances of Jason's conception, though he'd been living in Riversbend at the time. No doubt he imagined—like everyone else—that some local lad had been responsible. The only people who could have guessed were the van Aarks, but they'd been rarely at Strath-haven and Cassie had kept out of their way after Dan had left. She doubted they'd ever known of Jason's existence.

'Actually, I know him,' she said, standing up to begin stacking the plates. They'd been relaxing with a port after a long Sunday lunch. 'Met him years ago.'

'Really?' Roger's clear grey eyes registered surprise. And interest. 'Do tell.'

'Nothing much to tell,' Cassie shrugged, and continued to gather the crockery. 'He was a visitor at Strath-haven once, a few years back. I ran into him one day when I took some eggs down to Mrs Rambler. If you remember, she used to cook for the van Aarks sometimes.'

'Hmm. . .' Roger turned back to stare through the window again, down at Strath-haven. 'McKay's his name, isn't it?'

'Yes, that's right.'

'Big businessman from Sydney.'

'So it seems.'

Roger turned with a cheeky smile. 'Unattached, too, from what I hear.'

Cassie gave him a sharp look. 'Now, Roger——'

He held up his hands in mock defence, spilling a few drops of port. 'Oops! Joan, love, I. . .er. . .'

Joan swooped with a serviette, quickly wiping the brown drops from the dusky pink carpet. 'Men!' she said, but indulgently.

When she stood up, Roger gave her a squeeze and a kiss. 'You couldn't manage without us, though, could you?'

Cassie turned away from their display of affection, an uncomfortable sensation twisting in her stomach.

'Mum! Mum!' Jason appeared in the doorway, his face bright with excitement. 'There's a red car

coming up our drive. One of those with the top
down. I think it's Dan driving it.'

'Dan?' Roger asked, puzzled. 'Who's Dan?'

Cassie did her best to ignore her thudding heart.
'He means Dan McKay, the man we were just
talking about.'

Now Roger was frowning. 'And Jason calls him
Dan?'

Cassie sighed and turned to her son. 'You go
out and meet him, love. I'll be there in a moment.'

The boy ran off.

'Dan and I were having a chat after the auction
yesterday when Mum and Jason turned up,'
Cassie explained. 'Dan seemed to take to Jason
and didn't want to be called Mr McKay, that's all.
No big deal.'

'Hmm. . .'

Cassie didn't like the way Roger was looking at
her. He was far too curious. And perceptive.

She produced a disarming smile. 'I'll just go and
see what he wants. You stay here and finish your
drink with Mum.'

Cassie hurried from the room before any more
awkward questions could be asked.

But she didn't hurry to meet Dan. Once out of
Roger's sight her legs ground to a halt, her whole
being shaking with a thousand jangling nerves.
She leant against the wall of the hallway and took
several deep breaths. It was little use. She was

still a mess. Yet she had known that Dan would come. . .eventually.

With a jolt she realised that she had sent her son out to be alone with his father. Dan could be saying *anything* to him!

It propelled her into action, and she raced along the hall, out on to the back porch, down the steps and literally into Dan's arms.

'My, my,' he drawled, reaching out to steady her. 'What a pleasant change to find you so anxious to see me.'

For a heart-stopping second, Cassie went totally blank. She stared down at the hands that were grasping her upper arms, then up into Dan's handsome, smiling face. With an inevitability that she found appalling, her body began to respond to his nearness, his touch. Heat suffused the surface of her skin as that insidious seed of suppressed longing burst into life once more.

How easy it would be to give in to it. So easy. All she had to do was sink against the hard broadness of his chest and lift her mouth to his.

Instead she wrenched out of his hold, angry more at herself than at Dan. But her tongue didn't seem to know the difference. 'Don't kid yourself!' she snapped. 'You're the last man on earth I want to see.'

'You mean this isn't for me?' he mocked, indicating her clothing.

Cassie looked down at the cream knitted suit which she had worn to church and kept on afterwards. It was the one time during her week that she discarded her jeans.

'You know very well that I wasn't expecting you today,' she flared, her fingers shaking as they nervously arranged the loose top over the matching skirt. Unfortunately, the smoothing down of the ribbed garment only emphasised the thrust of her full breasts, which at that moment felt embarrassingly swollen.

Dan's gaze followed her self-conscious actions. 'Weren't you?'

'Of course not!' Her cheeks flamed. 'We happen to have a visitor.'

His black eyes narrowed. 'Who?'

'My boss,' she informed, without thinking to add that he was shortly to be her stepfather as well. 'He came for Sunday lunch.'

'You must have a close working relationship to have your boss over during the weekend.'

Cassie thought she heard a nasty innuendo in the words. She gave a defiant toss of her head. 'Roger comes to lunch *every* Sunday! Not that that is any of your business, Dan McKay. What are you doing here, anyway? You weren't invited.'

His laugh was dry. 'Something told me not to wait for an invitation.'

She glared at him. 'I thought I told you to keep away from me.'

Anger, hot and strong, swept his features. 'Don't be such a little fool, Cassie!' he slammed back. 'You knew I wouldn't stay away. That's my son out there!' He indicated Jason with a sharp jerk of his head.

'For God's sake, Dan, be quiet. . .' Cassie darted a stricken look over his shoulder, relieved to see that Jason was fully occupied inspecting Dan's car. And what boy wouldn't be enthralled? Even Cassie could recognise a Mercedes sports coupé when she saw one.

Her eyes sliced back to Dan in agonised appeal. 'Please, Dan. . .'

He lifted a dark eyebrow. '*Please*, is it now? I thought from your attitude yesterday and just now that it was to be war between us!'

She groaned.

His face showed a guarded surprise. 'Not war?' he asked softly, almost seductively. His right hand lifted to lie gently against her cheek.

Instinctively she stiffened, her head jerking back, her nostrils flaring like those of a frightened horse.

His hand dropped, his mouth curling into a caustic grimace. 'I thought as much. I came here willing to be reasonable, willing to negotiate. But I'd be wasting my breath, wouldn't I, Cassie? You've got no intention of really sharing Jason with me. Your mind is firmly made up. I'm not to be trusted. I'm a bastard, through and through. And that's that!'

Dan's bitter resentment fuelled a similar emotion in Cassie. 'What the hell did you expect?' she muttered at him in a low, hoarse whisper. 'That you could come back after all these years and be welcomed with open arms? That you could wipe the slate clean with a few convenient half-truths?'

'I'll tell you what I expect,' he retorted. 'I expect you to at least have the decency to listen to me. I expect to be allowed a reasonable share of Jason's life, to have the opportunity to love him as a father has a right to love his son!'

Cassie could only stare at Dan in wide-eyed horror. The man was either mad or so consumed with his own importance that he couldn't recognise or appreciate the feelings of others. Didn't he have any concept of what he had done, seducing her with promises of love and marriage, then leaving her to find out after he had gone that he was a married man? Did he honestly think that she was going to expose her son to his brand of loving? What would happen when he tired of the experience, when he decided that being a father was hard work, when he took off back to the bright lights of Sydney?

'You have no rights, Dan McKay!' she spat at him. 'You gave away your rights nine years ago! And I warn you, if you hurt my son I'll——'

'*My*, son, too,' he broke in harshly.

'Only technically!'

He grabbed her. 'Is that my fault? How was I to know?'

'If you'd stayed around long enough, you would have found out, you. . .you. . .'

'Bastard?' Dan suggested.

'If the cap fits, wear it!'

His hands fell from her arms. He drew himself up, stiff and tall, his eyes frightening in their steel-edged resolve. 'You won't give an inch, will you?'

Cassie looked into Dan's eyes and knew instinctively, overwhelmingly that she had made a ghastly mistake. She should have been more conciliatory, more reasonable, regardless of the circumstances. Aggression only bred aggression, and Dan was a wealthy, powerful man—a man not used to being crossed. It came to her with shocking clarity that if she kept blocking access to his son he might actually steal the boy. She had heard of fathers kidnapping their children and fleeing overseas. The very thought made her feel ill.

'Now let me warn *you*, Cassie Palmer,' he ground out, his voice vibrating with deadly menace. 'If you thought I was a bastard before, that's nothing to the bastard I'm going to be. You don't want me to tell Jason I'm his father, do you?'

Cassie caught her breath, once again glancing anxiously at her son. He was sitting behind the wheel of the sports car, making noises with his mouth, pretending to drive.

'But I will do exactly that if you don't do as I say. No one is going to keep me from my son, do you hear me? No one!'

And with that he spun round, striding away down the path. At the back gate, he whirled, setting incredibly cold eyes upon her. But when he spoke, his voice was amazingly normal. 'So glad you can drop in for a drink this evening, Cassie. . .I'll be looking forward to it. Say about eight? Your visitor should be gone by then. I know you won't be late. We have so much to talk about. . .' He cast a meaningful glance in Jason's direction, his threat quite clear.

Jason looked up, hearing Dan's last words. 'Can I come too, Dan?'

'Sorry, son,' he said gently. 'Only grown-ups allowed. Besides, don't you have to go to school tomorrow?'

Jason's face dropped. 'Yeah. . .' He climbed out of the car, eyes down.

'Don't you like school?'

'I s'pose it's all right.'

'You can come over to my place after school tomorrow, if you like.'

The boy's face brightened. 'That'll be super!' He ran to his mother. 'Can I, Mum?'

She looked over his head at Dan's uncompromising expression. 'As long as you're home before dark,' she managed to get out.

'Wow! Terrific!'

'I'll pick you up from school, Jason,' Dan suggested smoothly. He lifted an eyebrow at Cassie. 'I'm sure he'd like a ride in my car.'

Cassie's insides tightened. She didn't want her son left alone with Dan, but what else could she do? If she said no it might make the situation worse.

She glared at the man whom she had once loved. He was a stranger—a dark, malevolent stranger. Hatred welled up in frightening swirls. Bitter, hot hatred.

His mouth pulled back into a sardonic smile, terrifying her. For he had seen her hatred. And was unmoved by it.

'See you tonight, then,' he called nonchalantly. 'And tomorrow afternoon for you, my boy,' he added, ruffling Jason's hair before striding through the gate and round the nose of the car. He opened the driver's door, pausing to give Cassie a farewell salute before sliding behind the wheel.

It was a mocking, almost threatening gesture, impelling Cassie to place a protective arm around Jason's slender shoulders. The engine purred into life and Cassie caught a glimpse of a harsh glance before the red car disappeared.

Only then did she draw breath. How could she still want such an individual? What devilish fate made her respond to his touch, and no other man's?

'Dan's real nice, isn't he, Mum?' Jason said with a happy, upturned face. 'I like him.'

Cassie's heart contracted. What an impossible situation she was caught in! 'He likes you, too, love,' she said truthfully.

'I can't wait till tomorrow. Hey, Gran!' He ran into the house, bursting with his news.

Cassie felt close to despair as she watched her son run off. Nine years she had spent making life happy and secure for her son. Nine long, hard years! It had not been easy being an unmarried mother in Riversbend; it had not been easy returning to university to finish her degree. But she had done it. She had got on with her life and made a success of it. She was a respected member of the community, and Jason was a happy, well-adjusted boy.

Dan was threatening everything she held dear.

And, much as she hated the man and what he was doing, she had handled him very poorly. Her blatant lack of co-operation had made him resort to a type of blackmail. Of course, she could go down to Strath-haven tonight and apologise profusely, then beg Dan to see things her way. But would he respond to such an appeal? He was angry. No. . .furious! He wasn't going to listen to her. She just knew it.

With a groan she turned round to walk back up

the path, her mind still revolving. What weapon did she have, what argument could she use to sway this angry man?

And then it came to her. . .slowly. . . insidiously.

Cassie stopped at the base of the porch steps, her mouth suddenly dry. Could she do it? Dared she do it?

'Cassie. . .'

She blinked and looked up. Joan was frowning down at her, Roger at her elbow.

'Jason says he's going over to Dan's tomorrow after school,' Joan said. 'Is that right?'

Cassie swallowed. 'Yes, it is.'

'He also said something about you going down to Strath-haven tonight.'

Cassie could see that Roger was all ears. 'That's right. He's asked me down for a drink this evening,' she said truthfully.

'Well, well,' Roger beamed. 'And what did you say?'

'Yes, of course.'

If Cassie hadn't been so distracted she might have laughed at Roger's surprise, for it had been years since she'd accepted a date with a man.

CHAPTER SIX

CASSIE stepped over to the full-length mirror behind her bedroom door and stared into it. She turned sideways to inspect a rear view, and groaned.

'Dear God, I can't wear this,' she muttered. 'It's disgusting!'

She turned back to face the front, her eyes travelling once again over the figure-hugging red woollen sheath. It had been bought several years ago when she had been very thin, and the material now had to stretch to fit, so that, while the neck-to-knee, long-sleeved style was quite modest, the effect once it was moulded to her shapely body was suggestive in the extreme.

Cassie had merely wanted to look attractive, not like a scarlet woman. Her mother had suggested the dress, and the colour did look well on her, but its present effect was far too obvious, much too sexy!

But isn't that what you need to look like? an inner voice taunted.

A fluttering spasm claimed Cassie's stomach at the thought of trying to vamp Dan McKay. She hoped and prayed that such a drastic solution

would not be ncessary. It worried her terribly
what might happen to her if she did follow that
course. What if things got out of hand? *She* might
become the victim, not him, for much as she hated
him she couldn't deny that she wanted him, too.
And he made love so very very well. . .

Cassie spun away from the mirror and began to
pace the room, talking to herself all the while.
She would definitely try eating humble pie first.
She would tell him that he could see Jason as
much as he wished, provided he didn't reveal his
parentage. She would explain the difference
between life in a country area and the vast,
impersonal nature of a city existence. The man
was not heartless, surely? Even if he didn't give a
damn for her feelings, he would probably listen to
reason over matters relating to Jason.

She could point out how their son would be
terribly hurt by the comments of unthinking
people, not to mention those made by the other
children at school. Kids could be very cruel.

Yes, she would try to reason with the man. . .at
first.

And if that didn't work?

Cassie stopped pacing.

If reason didn't work, she decided with a surge
of grim determination, she *would* try to capitalise
on the sexual attraction between them. She didn't
have to sleep with the man, merely string him
along a little—anything to diffuse the situation, to

give her some power over him, some weapon to wield. Maybe it was wrong to promise and then not deliver, but. . .

She firmly pushed aside any feelings of guilt. Dan should have known better than to threaten the security of her child. Cassie was prepared to do anything to protect Jason's happiness, even if it meant swallowing her pride, throwing away her personal dignity; even if it meant putting herself fairly and squarely into the lion's den.

A knock at her door interrupted the silent tirade of resolutions.

'Cassie? Can I come in?'

'Just a moment.' She pulled out a black thigh-length cardigan, dragging it over the sexy red dress. She didn't want her mother to jump to conclusions, even right ones. 'Come in,' she called, her heart racing.

'Cassie, I. . .' Her mother stopped and frowned. 'Won't you be hot in that cardigan?'

Cassie picked up a hairbrush and gave a good imitation of nonchalance, talking and brushing at the same time. 'It's going to be chilly in the jeep.' She flicked back her fringe and smoothed the rest into its natural pageboy style, deliberately not looking at her face. She didn't want her to see the over-bright blue eyes, or the parted lips, trembling in scarlet gloss. 'I'll take the cardigan off once I get there,' she added, swallowing a lump of panic at the thought.

Her mother was staring down at her stockinged feet. 'What shoes are you going to wear?'

Cassie had pulled out a pair of outrageously high red sandals which she'd bought one year at a sale. But after putting the dress on she'd changed her mind. 'My black flatties, I guess.'

'Your black flatties?' her mother repeated. 'In *that* dress?' She spied the red sandals near the bed and picked them up. 'What's wrong with these? I mean. . .it's not as if you're a tall girl, Cassie. Though it wouldn't matter next to a man like Dan.'

Cassie said nothing. But she knew better than to argue with her mother over matters of dress. She put down the hairbrush and reluctantly slipped on the shoes.

Joan smiled smugly at her daughter. 'You'll knock him dead, darling.'

Cassie's sigh betrayed her jagged nerves. 'Mum. . .you know I'm only going down to talk to the man.'

Her mother's face assumed one of her innocent expressions. 'Of course you are. . . Here. . .' And she picked up the bottle of Paradise perfume lying on the dressing-table, giving Cassie a liberal spray.

Cassie had to laugh. 'Mum, you are an incurable romantic.' And, curling an arm around her mother's elbow, Cassie shepherded her from the room.

'Thanks for looking after Jason for me,' she

said as they walked along the hallway. 'And don't let him talk you into letting him watch the Sunday movie.'

'Would I do that?'

'Yes! That boy can twist you around his little finger.'

Her mother's smile faded. 'You know, Cassie, I'm going to miss the little minx when Roger and I get married.'

'Now, Mum, don't start that. You know it's time you made a life for yourself. And it's not as if you're going to be far away. Riversbend town is less than three miles from here and you can come out any time. Besides, didn't we agree that Jason would go to your place in town after school each afternoon till I've finished work?'

'Yes. . .'

'Well, then, you'll still see plenty of each other.'

As the two women passed the lounge doorway, Cassie popped her head inside. Jason was watching *The Cosby Show* and laughing with the uninhibited joy of a child.

'I'm going now, Jason,' she called. 'Be a good boy for your Gran, and don't forget to clean your teeth.'

He swung round from where he was sitting cross-legged on the floor and smiled at her. Cassie's heart contracted at the sight of those dancing black eyes. Never had he looked so much like his father, and it was disturbing. How long would it be before some eagle-eyed gossip made the connection? Particularly if Dan started being seen in Jason's company in public.

The drive down to the suspension bridge gave her more time to think. And to worry.

Suddenly she wished she had not worn the red dress. It had been a stupid thing to do. And precipitate, being too blatantly sexy. How could she mediate the situation first with an ounce of dignity and common sense looking as she did?

The jeep reached the riverbank too quickly for Cassie's liking. She pulled up next to the bridge, sick with apprehension at what lay ahead. She prayed that Dan *would* be reasonable, for every tentacle of her intuition was screaming that to invite Dan to make love to her in any way at all would be to invite disaster!

Extracting herself from behind the wheel in the ridiculously tight skirt proved difficult, though it made Cassie all the more determined to keep the cardigan on. She reassured herself as she struggled up the steps on to the moonlit bridge that a cardigan didn't look all that strange. The evening was clear and cool, a breeze coming off the river. Time enough to remove the covering garment later—if the need arose.

The house looked eerie in the moonlight, with only a few of the many windows showing a light. Cassie hesitated at the base of the stone steps, apprehension gnawing at her stomach. If it hadn't been for Jason she would have turned tail and run.

She put one nervous foot forward, then froze. A Dobermann, sleek and powerful, awaited her at the top of the stone steps, growling with teeth bared. She kept very still, her thudding heart appreciative of the breed's reputation, though she had never encountered one in all her years as a country vet.

She knew not to show fear with an animal, but the hairs on her neck were prickling ominously.

'Sit!' she tried in her most authoritative voice.

No change. If anything, the dracula-like teeth were bared even more.

Cassie swore under her breath. Where was Dan? He was expecting her, wasn't he? It was already ten past eight.

'Why don't you sit, you rotten dog?' she hissed. 'Or go away.'

'Maybe he justs wants to look at you.' A voice emerged from the blackness, along with its owner. 'Back, Hugo!' he commanded, and the dog disappeared.

Dan stood at the edge of the veranda, his impressively male body silhouetted against the rectangle of light falling from the open front door. Cassie caught her breath. He was as sleek and dark as the dog had been, yet infinitely more dangerous, his satanic image enhanced by the clothes he was wearing. Black shoes, black trousers, a black polo-necked sweater.

Cassie felt hopelessly intimidated, as well as a ghastly sexual awareness. Both reactions irritated her.

'Are you coming up?' Dan drawled. 'Or do we talk out here with the mosquitoes?'

'There are no mosquitoes in September,' she countered tartly.

He gave a mock salute. 'I bow to your judgement, Madam Vet.'

Cassie stiffened. 'How did you know I was a vet? Have you been questioning people about me?'

His sigh carried frustration. 'You really are paranoid, aren't you? Perhaps I just assumed it, my sweet. You told me nine years ago you were doing a veterinary science degree, don't you remember?'

Oh, yes. . . She remembered. She remembered *all* the things she had told him, all the intimate, loving, soul-destroying things!

A resurgence of bitterness had her glaring up at him, but he didn't appear to notice. Or maybe he couldn't see her properly in the shadows. Either way he ignored her angry look and stretched one hand towards her. 'Come. You're beginning to irritate me, standing down there like a reluctant virgin on her wedding night.'

Cassie clamped her teeth together, biting back

a sharp retort. It was going to be hard to keep control of her temper, she realised with some dismay. She had to remember to be very pleasant.

Nevertheless, she ignored Dan's outstretched hand, negotiating the steps as carefully as possible in the ridiculously high heels. 'You'll have to do something about that dog of yours,' she said thoughtfully as she reached the veranda, 'if you expect me to let Jason come to visit.'

Dan's laughter chilled her soul. Cassie stared at him, unable to hide her alarm. 'Why are you laughing? I haven't said anything funny.'

His mouth snapped shut, then creased back in a humourless smile. 'It was the choice of the word "*let*" that I found amusing. Come. . .I'm tired of this stupid banter. We'll go into the library and get down to real business.'

With that he took her elbow, propelling her as he had the previous afternoon through the doorway, along the hall then into the library, his touch no less disturbing than on that occasion.

The door closed ominously behind them. Then, before Cassie could stop him, Dan slipped the black cardigan from her shoulders. 'You'll be too hot in this,' he pronounced.

She spun round, her cheeks reddening. But he hadn't noticed her dress yet. He was walking away from her to hang the garment over a chair near the door. Cassie glanced around the room, wondering where she could stand to make her choice of clothing less. . .obvious.

But there was nowhere.

She couldn't very well hide behind the heavy green curtains or the large walnut desk. Otherwise, the only furniture consisted of four deeply cushioned armchairs, whose backs were hard against the bookshelves. Even the drinks cabinet was built-in.

Stricken, she stared down at the pale gold carpet, which was thick and plush underfoot, trying desperately to find the courage to meet Dan's eyes. Once again she had underestimated something. This time her own pride. She knew— no matter what the motivation—that she could not belittle herself by trying to even mildly seduce this man. Yet he would be bound to suspect something, once he looked at her dress!

When she did finally glance up it was to find Dan staring at her, as she had expected. But not with a knowing leer. More a black, brooding anger.

'Going somewhere, Cassie?' he grated out. 'Or have you already been.'

Relief overwhelmed her. Here was the perfect excuse for her appearance, supplied by Dan himself.

'I have a late date' she returned, adopting a nonchalant manner. 'I didn't think I'd be here all that long.'

The black eyes blazed. Surely he couldn't be

jealous? she thought dazedly. The thought brought a swift, mad pang of pleasure.

'I suppose it's your boss again. What was his name? Roger? I do hope he's a patient man,' Dan added caustically. 'This might take some time.'

'He'll wait!' she snapped, perversely not telling him the truth. For some deep, dark reason that even Cassie didn't want to explore, she liked Dan sounding jealous.

'I dare say.' His eyes travelled over her body with insolent slowness, lingering first on her thighs, then drifting up to her full, taut breasts. 'A body like yours would be worth waiting for. From what I can see—which is ample—it's even better than I remembered.'

Cassie felt totally mortified. He might as well have touched her, so intense was her response to his scrutiny, his words. Heat suffused her skin. An unnerving excitement ran through her veins. 'I am more than a body, Dan McKay,' she protested, but far, far too shakily. 'I have a mind. And feelings!'

His laughter was mocking. 'I must apologise. It's hard to remember such esoteric matters when confronted by such a striking. . .dress.' His eyes slid down her legs to her feet. 'Not to mention the shoes.'

She assumed a stony mask, brilliantly covering up her fluster. 'I am not here to discuss my appearance. Or my love-life. I think we should get to the point.'

'Very well.' Dan turned abruptly and strode around behind the desk. He sat down in the leather swivel-chair, leaning back, elbows on the arms, fingers linked in front of his chest. His black gaze studied her mercilessly for several elongated seconds, making her feel lost and vulnerable.

'Do sit down, Cassie,' he said at last. 'If you can manage it.'

The prospect of sinking into one of the deep armchairs, her skin-tight skirt riding up dangerously, rattled her. 'I'd rather not, thank you.'

'Suit yourself.'

She walked over to stand next to the long windows, staring blankly out on to the moonlit island. When her gaze landed on the outline of the river studio she closed her eyes. Tight.

'Remembering, Cassie?' Dan asked, in an oddly tender voice.

Her eyes flew open. 'Remembering what?' she snapped, whirling round to face him.

Undeterred by her sharp tone, he went on. 'What we once shared. . . Remember the time you came to me at the studio in the middle of the night, unable to sleep. How you slipped into my bed, naked and ready. How——'

'Stop it!' she lashed out, alarmed at the way his words were arousing her. 'I didn't come down here tonight to be tormented by you, Dan McKay.

I came here to discuss my. . .to discuss Jason. Nothing else. The last thing in the world I want is to be reminded of my stupid adolescent behaviour with you!'

She glared at him, her face coldly angry. But her hands were trembling, her pulse was pounding, her mind a chaotic mass of erotic memories. Memories of hot summer nights and moonlit swims, of hungry kisses and bodies blending, of passionate possession. . .and blissful surrender.

He stood up, and began walking around the desk, coming her way. Cassie froze. Dear God, don't let him touch me. . .

He didn't. Instead, he walked over to the cocktail cabinet and poured himself a drink. Straight Scotch, by the look of it. He didn't even bother to add any ice from the bucket resting at his elbow. Lifting the glass, he downed the amber-coloured liquid in one swallow, then turned to face her, eyes sardonic.

'Forgive my rudeness. I should have asked you what you were drinking these days.'

'I don't drink. You know that.'

One eyebrow lifted. 'All I know, my dear, is that you didn't drink once. But things have changed, haven't they? You've changed. The girl I remember would never have made a date with one man, intending to slink off afterwards to meet another.'

Cassie flinched inwardly, but refused to take

the bait. 'You call this. . .meeting. . .a date? Do I have to remind you that you blackmailed me into coming here tonight?'

Dan smiled coldly as he refilled the glass. 'All's fair in love and war,' he pronounced, then drained that drink as well.

He even poured a third. But this time he added ice and carried it back to the desk. His sigh was heavy as he slumped back in the chair. Cassie felt an unexpected and annoying wave of sympathy for him. He looked so bleak as he stared at her over the rim of the glass.

'Tell me, Cassie,' he said at last, 'what mischance caused you to fall pregnant with Jason in the first place? Did you forget to take the Pill one night? Was that it?'

Cassie sighed. She should have known that he would ask that. He was far too intelligent to forget. 'I wasn't on the Pill,' came the reluctant admission.

The glass of whisky hovered at his lips and he slowly lowered it to the desk. His eyes hardened. 'But you said you were?'

'No. . .I didn't.'

He leant forward. 'I remember—clearly—that first time. I asked if it was safe. You reassured me that it was perfectly safe. I assumed that meant that you were on the Pill as a general precaution.'

Cassie sighed. 'I realise that's what you thought. . .'

Silence descended.

Finally Dan spoke again, in a careful, almost wary tone. 'Were you deliberately trying to get pregnant, Cassie?'

Her eyes rounded. 'No!'

'Then why. . .why take such a risk?'

She shrugged despairingly. It would be useless to tell him how obsessive her feelings had become. How the first few times it *had* been relatively safe, but as the days had worn on and the risk had increased, she hadn't been thinking straight any more. She hadn't been able to help herself. All she'd been able to think of was Dan loving her, Dan possessing her, Dan. . . Dan. . . Dan. . .

'I was stupid,' she admitted grimly, and closed her eyes again, trying not to remember, but failing miserably.

A light touch on her cheek jerked her eyes open to find Dan standing in front of her. How had he moved so silently, so swiftly? She stared up into his face, taken aback that his expression mirrored an unexpected tenderness. 'No,' he said gently. 'Not stupid. . .just a woman in love.'

He was too close, Cassie thought breathlessly. Much too close. 'In love, Dan?' she scoffed, and took a step back. 'Hardly that, I think. Infatuated, perhaps. But not love. No. . .not love.'

Her cold denial affected him. She could see that. His nostrils flared wide. An angry muscle twitched along his jaw. 'And are you infatuated with this boss of yours?'

Cassie tossed off a careless laugh. 'For heaven's sake, Dan. I'm twenty-nine years old. Past the age of infatuation, surely?'

'It's just sex, then.' A statement. Not a question.

'Maybe I'm in love,' she tossed at him. Any thought of Jason had vanished. All Cassie wanted to do was lash out, to assuage some of her own personal pain and agony.

He grabbed her so quickly and so roughly that she gasped in pain. 'That's not true!' he ground out, his rasping breath only inches from her own. 'I know that for a fact. And do you know why? You're incapable of it! Your soul is so twisted and warped with bitterness, you've forgotten what love is. You're too full of hate!'

Suddenly his hands fell away from her arms, but a dangerous smouldering still remained in his gaze. It held Cassie, leaving her breathless and weak. When his right hand came up to cup her chin she did not pull away. She stared back at him, stunned into a dazed submission.

'Do let's be honest, my darling,' he drawled in a low, sensual voice. 'It's lust, not love, that drives you into that man's bed. You're a very sexy woman, Cassie Palmer—incredibly easy to turn on. Do you think I didn't notice the way you responded to me yesterday? Me. . .a man you despise. I dare say that if you hadn't remembered who was kissing you I could have taken you here, in this room, either on the desk or on the floor.'

His smile was cruelly knowing. 'That's lust, my lovely. And lust is a very transferable emotion. *Very* transferable!'

His hand slid down her throat, down over a single swollen breast, down over her ribs till it stopped on her quivering stomach.

Cassie sucked in a ragged breath through dry, parted lips. Why don't I do something? she asked herself dazedly. Why don't I stop him?

The hand moved again, this time sliding across then up over the curve of her hip to rest at her waist. 'You're trembling, Cassie,' he whispered harshly. 'Do you tremble for Roger so easily? Or is it only for me. . .?'

She almost said it, almost made her ghastly confession. Her lips actually opened, the words already forming. *Only for you. . . Only for you. . .*

His kiss smothered them totally, utterly, and, while Cassie's first instinct was to shut her mouth, to struggle, it was short-lived. From the moment his arms moved to enfold her close against him, the battle was lost. She groaned under his passionate onslaught, and slowly, inexorably, her lips parted, allowing his tongue the entry it so clearly desired. A sound growled deep in his throat, arousing her with its primitive, animal quality.

Her own tongue moved foward, quite instinctively, but when it slid into Dan's mouth she was not prepared for the explosion of passion she had so unwittingly unleashed.

His arms tightened around her till she could barely breathe, his tongue thrusting deep into her mouth in a savage, primitive rhythm. On and on went the kiss till Cassie's head was whirling, till her limbs were like jelly, till her body was a lifeless, malleable object moulded to Dan's in blatant sensuality. Chest was fused to chest, stomach to stomach, thigh to thigh.

Finally, he did take his mouth away, sliding swollen lips across her cheek till he found her ear. The tip of his tongue traced a wet path around the shell before dipping inside again and again, making Cassie shiver with sheer electric pleasure.

Her head fell backwards, offering up her throat to his ministrations, and when he took it, sucking the throbbing flesh at the base with hot, hungry lips, she groaned.

The sound brought his mouth back to hers in yet another kiss, this one even more feverish than the first. Blood began roaring in Cassie's ears. Liquid fire gushed along her veins. She was in another world, a crazy, ecstatic world where the senses swam, where time was suspended, where her only desire was to remain in Dan's arms.

She was dimly aware of his hands relaxing their

hold to run up and down her back, but when he began rubbing her softness against the hard muscle of his manhood Cassie's pleasure gradually changed to an aching, escalating tension. It wasn't enough to have his mouth fused to hers. It wasn't enough to have his hands on her. It wasn't nearly enough.

She wanted to feel him moving deep inside her. She wanted the release that only his total possession could give. And even as she wished it her own body started to move, writhing against him in an invitation as old as time.

Dan pulled back for a second, his eyes wide with passion and wonder, and then he was drawing her down on to the carpet, stretching out beside her. He kissed her again, one of his hands sliding down her taut, eager body, down to her knee then slowly up, up her softly trembling thigh.

She arched against him, tense, expectant, her whole being concentrating on his hand, which was moving inexorably closer to the hot, molten core of her desire.

The door of the library opened.

'Mr McKay, I knocked, but you didn't. . .'

Cassie almost died. She wrenched her mouth away and gaped over Dan's shoulder. The intruder was a complete stranger to her. He was no more than twenty-five and might have been good-looking under the red face. 'Hell! I. . .I'm terrible sorry, Mr McKay, I——'

'Get out of here!' Dan growled, his stiffened body held rigidly above her. 'And close the bloody door on your way out!'

CHAPTER SEVEN

THE door shut with the force of an earth tremor.

Cassie's stricken gaze swung to Dan. But his eyes were squeezed tight, his face twisted in a type of anguish. He shuddered and expelled a long-held breath. 'God,' he muttered.

Cassie groaned as she thought of the picture they must have presented to their unexpected visitor. Another couple of seconds and Dan would have been. . .

Embarrassment brought a blast of heat into her cheeks. Upset and flustered, she tried to move.

Dan's hands whipped up to her shoulders and pinned her to the carpet. 'No!' he ground out, wild black eyes flying open.

She shook her head frantically and kept trying to escape, but her wriggling movements were futile. And their effect disastrous. Her swollen breasts accidentally rubbed against Dan's chest, rekindling the smouldering fire in his eyes. Seeing his reaction, she stupidly struggled harder, trying to slide away from under his hands, this tactic only serving to make her tight skirt ride dangerously high.

He swore under his breath, hot eyes fixed on

the tips of her breasts jutting provocatively against the thin woollen material. His breathing grew disconcertingly rapid, his chest rising and falling in a ragged rhythm.

'Dan. . .please. . .let me up,' she gasped.

His eyes snapped up to her face. 'Damn it all, Cassie, ignore that! He won't come back. He wouldn't dare! You can't want me to stop now. . .'

Cassie tried to speak, to object, but when his lips descended to devour the soft flesh of her throat her voice died. And when they moved down to a single swollen breast she could no longer even breathe.

His mouth opened and closed around its prey, the moist heat within quickly saturating the layers of material covering the nipple. She could feel his teeth against the sensitised peak, nipping it into even further arousal. More and more it responded to him, growing harder and larger, till the sensations became unbearable.

'No. . .' she objected. But feebly, without conviction.

'Yes,' he grated back.

Her wide blue eyes were drawn to the library door. She imagined that man, standing outside, listening, smiling, sniggering. 'No!' she screamed, and slapped Dan hard on the side of the head.

Glazed black eyes jerked up to stare at her.

'I said *no*!' she repeated, with gritted teeth this time.

Gradually, the almost incoherent quality in Dan's gaze faded, to be replaced by a brooding, barely controlled fury. He was still breathing hard and his hands were brutal in their hold around her hips.

For one terrifying moment Cassie feared that he would continue. And the horrible thing was, she knew that it would not be rape. Her body still wanted him, quite desperately. He only had to push the issue and she was his.

'Let me up,' she demanded. And held her breath.

After an excruciating couple of seconds, Dan shrugged and rolled away, a scornful smile curling his lips. 'It's a lady's privilege to change her mind,' he drawled as he got up. 'But you do realise, Cassie, that you're only delaying the inevitable.'

Cassie struggled to her feet. She was fiercely aware of the clammy material pressed against her breast, still wet where his mouth had been. Shame curled in her stomach. She had been so easy. . .

And while Dan's words had a ghastly ring of truth about them, they evoked a proud and defiant anger in her.

Her chin tilted upwards. 'Don't count your chickens, Dan. You're not dealing with the same silly naïve girl you seduced nine years ago.'

His face tightened. 'That much is obvious, my

dear. If I remember correctly, we had known each other. . .ten days, wasn't it?. . .before we became lovers. By your response tonight I think we'll be a lot quicker this time, don't you?'

His mocking disdain cut Cassie to the quick. Her only wish was to strike back, to hurt him as he was hurting her. 'Aren't you forgetting one small matter, Dan? I already have a lover—a lover who's waiting for me at this very moment, only too willing to meet my physical needs. I certainly don't need you!'

Cassie shrank back from the frightening force of his glare.

'You are not to go to this man tonight. Do you hear me, Cassie? Or any other night. I forbid it!'

Her laughter was almost hysterical. 'You forbid it? *You* forbid it? And who do you think you are, Dan McKay, forbidding me to do anything?'

He smiled.

Cassie rocked back. Never had she encountered a smile like it. Thin and cruel; edged in pure steel.

He turned and walked slowly round behind the desk, seating himself again and leaning back in the chair, looking up at her with cynically cold eyes. Cassie found his silence more threatening than the loudest tirade.

'I'll tell you who I am, Cassie Palmer,' he said at last. 'I am the father of your son. I am also an extremely rich man. But more than either of those things, I am a man who has had a gutful of

sacrifices and compromises and considerations. I
want my son. And, strange as it may seem, I still
want you. . .' the corners of his mouth lifted in a
dry, ironic smile '. . .even if you aren't the same
girl I fell in love with. Nevertheless, you are a
very desirable woman—a woman I have a mind
to possess. Or should I say repossess? And before
you tell me so, I'm well aware that you despise
me now. Nevertheless, I am quite capable of living
with that, as long as you give me what I want.'

Cassie's head was spinning. 'And what is that?'
she asked shakily. 'Sex?'

His face remained stony. 'Among other things.'

'What other things?'

'My son, for starters. And not on any part-time,
neighbourly basis. I want him here, in my home,
all the time.'

'But I don't want——'

'I don't give a damn what you want!' he
slammed at her, jumping to his feet and banging
his fist down on the desk. 'You've lost all chance
of my considering your wishes. I will not be
treated like some vermin that's just crawled out
from under a stone!'

Cassie quaked under the force of his fury. Dan
had said he could be ruthless, but even she had
not envisaged something like this.

'No matter what you thought of me,' he went
on brutally, 'you should not have kept me in
ignorance of my son. Maybe there was some

excuse nine years ago, but yesterday, when I told
you my wife was dead, when I showed I still cared
about you, you should have told me the truth.
That would have been the decent thing to do!'

'But, Dan, I——'

'Enough! You wouldn't listen to my expla-
nations then. I'm not interested in yours now.'

Cassie didn't know what to do, what to say. She
was totally confused, frantically upset. 'I. . .I
wanted to tell you,' she blurted out. 'When Jason
was born it nearly killed me not to contact you.'

'Then why didn't you?' His voice was cold,
unmoved. 'My name is listed in the phone book.'

'I. . .we. . . Mum and I hadn't told my father
that you were responsible. He was so angry about
my pregnancy. Mum thought it better he think it
was some boy at a party one night. If he'd found
out I'd had an affair with a. . .a married
man. . .God knows what he would have done.'

'Come now, Cassie, you don't expect me to
believe you were protecting *me* all this time?'

His derision brought utter frustration. 'No, of
course not! It was to protect my father! He had a
heart condition. Not that my keeping my affair
with you a secret was any benefit in the end,' she
said bitterly. 'Shortly after Jason was born Dad
had an attack and died. And it was all my fault.
Mine and yours! I hated you then, don't you see?
And when you came back yesterday, smiling at
me as though the past was nothing, I. . .I. . .' She

fumbled for words. Everything was so mixed up in her head. She did still hate him, didn't she?

'You hated me even more,' Dan finished for her in a matter-of-fact tone. 'Yes, Cassie, I do see. Love turning to hate is a common enough occurrence. But it doesn't change a thing, because, love me or hate me, you're going to marry me.'

All the breath was punched from Cassie's body. 'Marry you?' she gasped.

Dan's smile was dry. 'I can see my proposal has come as a shock. Perhaps I should give you some time to consider it.'

Cassie swallowed. 'How. . .how much time?'

'Twenty-four hours.'

'Twenty-four hours?' she repeated blankly.

'Must you repeat everything I say?' Dan ground out irritably. 'When you come to pick Jason up tomorrow, you can give me your answer.' He sat back down, then glanced up, eyes and face hard. 'Of course, I should explain what will happen if you refuse.'

Cassie said nothing. She was incapable of speaking.

'Jason is my son. A simple DNA test will prove that. What's more, I am a father willing and able to support his son very well. Oddly enough, courts these days don't favour the woman in custody cases as much as they used to. I have no doubt that I will get a fair hearing, which is more than I got from you.'

'You'd try to take my son away from me?' Cassie cried in a choked voice. Her throat was dry, her heartbeat suspended from fear.

Was that a trace of pity she saw pass across his face?

'Only if you force me, Cassie,' he said evenly.

Cassie whirled away, her hands coming up to cradle her cheeks. 'If *I* force *you*?' she cried. 'Oh, God. . .'

She whirled back, tears pricking her eyes, but renewed defiance in her heart. She strode over to the desk and leant on it, her face flushed and angry. 'You would have to be the most heartless man in the world, Dan McKay, not to mention the most stupid! Do you honestly think any court in the world would award you custody of my son? Even if the unthinkable happened, even if you somehow bribed your way to a favourable decision, you wouldn't win in the end. Jason would hate you for taking his mother away from him. Hate you, do you hear me? Almost as much as I hate you!'

Dan's knuckles showed white as he clenched the edge of the desk and pushed himself slowly to his feet. He loomed over her, his face and stance intimidating, but Cassie was too angry to be afraid.

'I'll fight you, Dan,' she threatened, glaring up

into his blazing eyes. 'I'll fight you every inch of the way, with every weapon I have. Even if you get Jason, you won't win!'

An electric silence enveloped them as they glowered at each other.

Surprisingly Dan was the first to look away. He turned and walked over to the window where he stood and stared into the night, his shoulders stiff, his whole stance incredibly tense. After several excruciating seconds, he turned to face Cassie, the set of his mouth tight and grim. 'I take your point,' he conceded grudgingly. 'That is not what I want. Not at all. I want Jason to love me.'

Cassie was swamped by such a wave of relief that she had to clutch the edge of the desk to steady herself.

'You would make a good adversary in the boardroom, Cassie Palmer,' Dan admitted. 'But don't underestimate your opponent. You haven't won yet.'

Her chest tightened. She should have known that this wouldn't be the end of the matter. Dan was not a man willing to lose. In anything.

The possibility of his kidnapping Jason again crossed her mind. As melodramatic as such an event seemed, people did do dreadful things when desperate. Cassie had to stop the situation from deteriorating to that level.

'I'm prepared to be reasonable about access,' she offered tautly.

Dan's expression remained guarded. 'Oh? In what way? As friend, or father?'

Cassie bit her bottom lip. 'I. . .I don't think it's wise to tell him you're his father just yet.'

'And why not?' The black eyes glinted dangerously. 'He doesn't think I'm dead, does he?'

'No. . .'

'Well, what does he think? What have you told him about me?'

'I. . . Not much. I explained that I didn't want to marry his father as I was too young, and that you lived too far away to visit.'

'And he accepts that?'

She shrugged. 'Jason's only eight. Perhaps in time he'll want more.'

'Why do you object to my telling Jason I'm his father?'

'This isn't the city, Dan. People around here are shockable. And narrow-minded. Jason would be hurt by the gossip.'

'And you? Would you be hurt by the gossip?'

Cassie drew herself up straight. 'I'd survive.'

Dan's expression was hard to read. Was it admiration? Or derision. . . 'I've no doubt you would,' he mocked, answering the question for her.

'You won't tell him?' she swept on, chin still up.

His hesitation in answering made her stomach

churn. 'I can't promise that, Cassie,' he finally admitted.

She almost stamped her foot. 'Damn you, Dan! Didn't you listen to what I said?'

'I do not live my life according to the opinions of others,' he snarled.

Her laugh was scornful. 'As well I know.'

'I don't blame you totally for wanting to turn the screw, Cassie,' he said in a low, deadly voice, 'but I'm warning you, don't keep doing it too long.'

She was about to speak, to challenge him, but common sense made her hold her tongue. Push him too far and who knew what he might do? At least he seemed to have dropped his ridiculous marriage proposal.

'What about tomorrow afternoon?' she asked, deliberately changing the subject. 'Do you still intend picking Jason up from school?'

'Yes.'

'You won't drive fast?'

'Of course not.'

'And he'll be safe in the helicopter?'

'For God's sake, Cassie!' Dan exploded. 'He's my son, too. I wouldn't dream of putting him at risk.'

Cassie believed him. Whatever else, Dan seemed to care about the boy. 'I. . .I'll tell him to wait for you at the bus-stop outside the school.

Do you know where the Riversbend primary school is?'

'I'll find it.'

'It's down a side-street. It——'

'I said I'd find it, Cassie. I've made my way successfully around the world several times. I don't need someone to hold my hand. Just you make sure you come personally to collect Jason, with your answer ready.'

'My answer? You mean. . .you still expect. . .?'

His expression was totally impassive. 'My proposal of marriage still stands, Cassie.'

'And if I say no?'

'I don't think you will, once you come to terms with the situation.'

Cassie gaped her astonishment.

'I'm sure you don't want Jason to be unhappy,' Dan went on, 'any more than I do.'

'How on earth can you——?'

'Do let me finish, my dear,' he cut in coldly.

She sighed her frustration, but let him continue.

'You say that telling Jason I'm his father just now is not in his best interests. I challenge that. I think Jason needs me. And he needs me now! Not in six months' or six years' time. How do you think he'll feel if and when you finally reveal the truth? Do you think he'll appreciate your reasons for delaying? Or that he'll believe you were only protecting him from gossip? There's bound to be gossip no matter when we tell him. Of course, the gossip would quickly die down, if you married me. . .'

'But I can't marry you!' Cassie exclaimed, her glare hiding her underlying paniic. 'I won't!' My God, to be with him every day, to sleep with him every night. . .

Dan's returning glare held no compromise at all. 'Let me assure you, Cassie, I'm not going to go away. And I will eventually tell the boy the truth. It is his right, after all. I must admit, I don't envy your position when I do.'

'What. . .what do you mean?'

'I wouldn't like having to explain to Jason why you refused to marry his father, especially after I vow my undying love for you both!'

'You'd lie to him?' she husked.

His jaw clenched. 'About what?'

'You might love Jason, but you don't love *me*, Dan McKay. Don't you dare say that you do!'

He said nothing.

'Why are you doing this?' she threw at him. '*Why*?'

He didn't even flinch. 'I'm doing what's best for Jason,' he declared in merciless tones. 'I expect you to do the same. If you truly love him. . .'

Cassie's whole body slumped, her eyes dropping to the floor in a gesture of defeat. It was useless, absolutely useless. The man was too hard. And too clever. Appealing to her motherly love was the lowest tack.

But very successful.

She didn't even react when he moved to stand in front of her, when his hands reached out to close firmly over her shoulders. All defiance was dead.

'Cassie. . .I don't want to hurt you. I never wanted to hurt you. . . But I will have my son. Make no mistake about that.'

Her eyes lifted—sad, weary eyes. 'All right,' she sighed.

He frowned down at her, tension seeping into his fingers. The tips pressed harder into her flesh. 'All right? What do you mean by that?'

'I mean all right, Dan.' Her voice was dull, flat. 'I'll do what you want. And you don't have to wait till tomorrow for your answer.'

'You mean you agree to marry me?' he asked in a surprisingly shocked tone. 'Just like that?'

'Yes.' She felt tired. Terribly tired.

'Even though you hate me?'

A deep, dark pain jabbed at her conscience. It found relief in a final burst of spirit. 'Does it matter?' she flung at him. 'I will do what I have to do. You said it earlier. I'm only putting off the inevitable. Once you tell Jason he's your son, he'll wonder why he can't have a normal family life like other children. What answer could I give him? So you see, Dan? There's no need for any more threats or more blackmail. You've won.'

'What about us?' he demanded.

'What *about* us?' she shot back.

'Goddamn you, Cassie, you know what I mean. It's not just the boy I want.'

Cassie's heart stopped beating.

'Don't imagine that I'll settle for a marriage of convenience,' he went on fiercely. 'I want you in my bed every night. I want you, all of you, body and soul.'

His arrogant demands found an answering fire in Cassie. She glared up at him, blue eyes flashing. 'We can't always have what we want, Dan. Do you imagine I *want* to marry you?'

'You still want me to make love to you. That much I know.'

She kept her chin held high. 'If I do, then I despise myself for it!'

'Don't say that!'

'Why not? It's true. Every time you touch me, down deep inside I cringe. My body might look to yours for a temporary relief, but afterwards. . .afterwards, Dan, I will only feel revulsion.'

'No!' he cried as she tried to pull free of him. His arms swept around her, holding her close, lifting her on to tiptoes till his lips were touching hers. 'You're wrong, Cassie,' he whispered into her mouth. 'Wrong. . . Hate has warped your mind. It could be wonderful. . .perfect. . .as it was before——'

'No,' she denied, fiercely trying to ignore his

lips brushing against hers. 'It will never be the same. Never! We don't love each other any more. When we go to bed now it will be having sex, not making love.'

'Call it anything you like!' he rasped, his fingers digging into her back. 'But don't delude yourself that it will be anything like the sex you've been having. Even now your body cries out instinctively for mine. You're trembling, Cassie. You want me. I was your first lover, your first real love. Nothing will change that, no matter how many men you've slept with since, no matter what that twisted soul of yours pretends. You were totally mine once and you will be again.'

'Never!' Cassie shook her head violently from side to side, all the while knowing that Dan was right. She might despise him as a person, but sexually she was still under his spell.

Quite abruptly he let her go, almost throwing her aside, stalking back over to the window and glaring through it in brooding silence.

When he whirled back to face her, Cassie was shocked by the raw, naked pain on his face. 'Well? What are you waiting for? Get out! Go to your blasted lover, for all I care! But understand this, Cassie Palmer. No wife of mine will lie in another man's bed. So you make it clear to your darling boss tonight that your affair is over! Terminated!' His eyes narrowed. 'If I ever find out differently. . .'

Cassie swallowed. An undercurrent of sexual revenge smouldered through Dan, making her fearful, yet at the same time disturbingly aroused.

'What. . .what about Jason?' she asked in a husky whisper. 'Do. . .do you still want me to pick him up from Strath-haven tomorrow? I could come after work, about five-thirty.'

'Do whatever you like,' he growled and spun away. 'Just get out of my sight.'

Cassie stared at the grim figure, a strange compassion stirring inside her. Dan was hurting, really hurting. It didn't matter to her that his jealousy came from a bruised ego, not true feeling. She wanted to go to him, to hold him, to tell him that there was no lover. But before she could even begin to move he rounded on her again, his face hard once more.

'Are you still here? What's the problem? Won't darling Roger have waited this long for you?' His mouth creased back into a cruel, taunting smile. 'Perhaps you've changed your mind, is that it? You want me to give your body that temporary release you spoke of. . .'

Cassie backed away, her eyes wide. When he took a step towards her she grabbed her cardigan and fled, Dan's wild, harsh laughter echoing in her ears.

CHAPTER EIGHT

CASSIE spent a terrible Monday. On the surface she functioned normally, going to work, operating all morning, making calls all afternoon, smiling and talking as though nothing was different. Underneath, she was a seething mass of confusion and fears. How could she have been so stupid as to agree to marry Dan? Whatever had possessed her?

The ever-observant Roger had frowned at her more than once, finally asking what was wrong, but she made some excuse about not sleeping well. He believed her because insomnia had been a recurring problem of Cassie's over the years.

Her mother had not been as easy to put off that morning at breakfast. She had been bursting with curiosity, wanting to know what had transpired with Dan. Cassie had no intention of telling her mother the blunt and embarrassing details of the entire evening. And Jason's presence at the breakfast table had precluded any open discussion about his father.

Cassie had, however, confessed reluctantly to her mother that Dan had asked her to marry him, not adding that she had already been emotionally blackmailed into saying 'yes'. She had let her mother think that the matter was yet to be decided. And, as far as Cassie was concerned in the cold light of day, that was so!

Joan had been astonished, then delighted, expressing the opinion that she was sure it would be for the best. 'After all, you've never really got over the man, have you?' she'd said perceptively. 'And I'm sure he must still care for you if he wants to marry you. Men these days don't marry merely because of an illegitimate child.'

Cassie did not have the heart to disillusion her. Jason was without doubt Dan's main motive for proposing marriage.

But he definitely did not care for her any more. He openly disliked the woman she'd become. Though for some perverse reason he still wanted her. His vow to reduce her to some sort of sexual slave was obsessive in its intensity, fuelled perhaps by a desire for revenge. Dan bitterly resented Jason's existence having been kept from him.

What terrified her most was how easily Dan would achieve his objective if she married him. And he expected her answer that afternoon!

By the time Cassie climbed into her jeep at the end of the day, she was emotionally exhausted. Quite automatically she turned on to the road for home instead of taking the highway which led to Strath-haven, and was half-way there before she realised her mistake. Shrugging wearily, she continued on, thinking to herself that it was just as well. She really couldn't face Dan looking as she did.

When she brought the jeep to a halt in front of the old farmhouse, Cassie was about to climb out from behind the wheel when she stopped. Why should she go inside and change? It was better that Dan saw her exactly as she was attired every workday. White overalls, no make-up, hair scraped back into a functional pony-tail. Maybe he would change his mind about marrying her, she thought wryly, if he saw her at her least attractive.

Cassie restarted the engine and drove down the hill towards the suspension bridge, detouring slightly to skirt Rosie's paddock. No untoward developments there, she thought with relief as she saw the mare actually cantering. Not that there should be. Foals rarely came early, but Rosie was getting on in years, which could make things slightly unpredictable. If anything went wrong at this late stage, Cassie worried. . .

I'm getting paranoid, she thought irritably. Rosie's as healthy as a horse! She laughed at her own pun and turned the jeep for the short run down to the river.

Jason must have been watching for her, for he raced to meet her as she stepped off the bridge, throwing his arms around her waist in an uncharacteristic hug. 'Gee, you're late. We thought you weren't coming. Dan was going to ring up Gran to find out what had happened to you, but I told him you'd make it sooner or later. I said you probably had a 'mergency with a cow or something.'

Cassie smiled down at her bright-eyed son as he skipped along the gravel path ahead of her, backwards, marvelling at his energy and thinking to herself that his happiness was really worth any sacrifice. But surely he could be happy, she frowned, without his mother making such a disastrous marriage?

'And guess what?' he was saying. 'I had three rides in the helicopter. But it's gone now, see?' he pointed to the spot on the front lawn where the machine usually stood. 'Dan sent it back to Sydney.'

Cassie glanced up then, having for some time been half-aware of Dan watching them from the veranda. Perhaps he was ensuring that she made no retreat now that she'd arrived.

'And which did you enjoy most?' she asked Jason, trying to keep her voice normal as they approached the front steps. 'The sports car?' She nodded towards the shining red Mercedes parked nearby. 'Or the helicopter?'

Jason said, 'The car was terrific, but the helicopter was super!'

Cassie's head snapped up to see Dan striding down the front steps of the house. Her breath caught in her throat seeing him at such close quarters, his very male frame dressed in blue jeans and a maroon shirt, the casual attire far more reminiscent of the Dan she had first met.

Made of faded denim, the jeans were tightly fitted, moulding his slim hips and powerful thighs. The long sleeves of the shirt were rolled up, the collar open at the neck. No watch or jewellery adorned his smooth, tanned flesh which drew Cassie's gaze like a magnet. Her insides tightened as she remembered how she used to run her hands over his hairless chest, loving the velvet feel of him.

Cassie blinked. What had Dan just said? She couldn't think.

Unnerved, she turned to her son. 'Ready to go home, Jason?' Even as the words popped out of her mouth she knew that she was acting like a fool. Dan would not let her go so easily. But the blistering sexual awareness he always evoked in her made Cassie want to run.

'Mrs Bertram is making us coffee,' Dan said smoothly. 'We can have it on the veranda and talk while Jason plays with Hugo.'

The enormous black dog must have heard his name, for he bounded around the corner. Cassie stiffened. 'Are you sure he——'

Her protest was cut off by the sight of her son

hugging the slavering Dobermann around the neck. The animal's huge tongue slurped up Jason's face, bringing squeals of objection. 'Oh, yuk! You sloppy old thing. Come on. . . Let's play fetch.' And the happy pair ran off.

'Don't concern yourself,' Dan reassured in a soft, kind voice. 'Once Hugo has been introduced to a person as a friend, he is devoted. He would protect Jason with his life now.'

Cassie could not help being surprised by Dan's pleasant manner. Where was the mocking devil of last night? 'Have. . .have you had the dog long?' she asked.

'Five years. Since he was a pup.'

'He's certainly a beautiful animal.' She kept watching the dog in the distance. It was safer than looking at Dan.

'He was Roberta's dog.'

Cassie's heart stopped. 'Roberta?'

Her eyes turned slowly to see Dan observing her closely. 'My wife,' he said evenly.

'Oh. . .' A chill came over Cassie. She didn't want to hear about Dan's wife. She couldn't bear to think that he had belonged to another woman all the time he'd been having an affair with her. A woman he had returned to and stayed with despite his talk about separation and divorce.

Mrs Betram's arrival with the coffee was timely.

She was a slim, efficient-looking woman of about fifty. Not a local. Cassie allowed Dan to

take her elbow and lead her silently up the steps
and over to the table set up on the veranda. The
coffee-service was exquisite—made of the finest
cream pottery. A selection of delicate pastries
rested on a serving plate.

Mrs Betram smiled at Cassie. 'And you'd be
Jason's mother?' the woman asked.

Dan stepped in and effected a proper introduction. Cassie could not help noticing the woman's
open curiosity about her. Or was it astonishment
that her boss was interested in such a country
bumpkin? She wished now that she had stopped
to improve her appearance.

'That's a lively lad you've got there,' Mrs
Betram commented as she poured the coffee.

Cassie chewed her bottom lip. 'He hasn't been
any trouble, has he?'

'Oh, good heavens, no!'

'He's had a whale of a time,' Dan added with a
laugh. 'But I think Paul was glad to go back to
Sydney.'

'Paul?' Cassie repeated enquiringly.

'My pilot.' Dan's eyes rested on Cassie in dry
amusement. 'You almost met him last night.
Thank you, Mrs Bertram, we can manage now.
Cream and sugar, Cassie?'

Cassie was glad of the woman's departure, for a
fierce blush was creeping up her neck. How could
Dan refer to such an embarrassing encounter so. . .
so casually? It was tactless. And tasteless. And

there she'd been thinking he'd turned over a new leaf!

'Yes, please,' she said stiffly. Then added, 'Mrs Bertram seems a nice person.'

'She is,' Dan agreed. 'Not that I've known her all that long. She's only been my housekeeper since Roberta died. Prior to that——'

'Do you have to keep referring to your first marriage?' Cassie flared.

Dan replaced the cream-jug with a sigh. 'Cassie. . .I want to explain. . .about Roberta——'

'But I don't want to hear,' she retorted wildly, knowing she was over-reacting, but finding it impossible to stop. 'I never want to hear about her. Never! Not if you want me to marry you!'

She raised furious eyes to his, almost daring him to continue, to ruin what he so obviously wanted. He glared back at her, his mouth setting into a thin, angry line.

'Right,' he bit out, and, with an abrupt movement, stood up and strode inside, returning shortly with a wad of papers and a biro. He pushed the coffee-cups aside and spread the sheets out on the table before her. 'You have to sign here.' He jabbed at some blank spaces on the forms. 'And here. This last one is an authority for my solicitor to pick up a copy of your birth certificate. Marriage licences require paperwork. And a special licence requires even more.'

She gulped, her earlier anger fading with the growing reality of the situation. This was not the past. This was here and now!

'We will be married on Sunday,' Dan was saying, 'here, in the garden. I'm flying in a celebrant from Sydney. There will be no guests other than your immediate family. Mine will not be attending. They all live in Perth. Too far to come at short notice. Here. . .' He picked up the biro and held it out for her.

Cassie took it with a trembling hand, then stared blankly down at the forms. Dan kept on talking in a rather cold, formal voice. At some stage he had sat down again.

'I imagine Mrs Bertram will be concerned about her position here when I inform her of our coming marriage. Shall I tell her she can stay, or do you prefer to run the house on your own? It's entirely up to you. Though I do strongly suggest that you consider keeping the staff on. They're reliable and discreet, and you'll need help when we entertain. As well as Mrs Bertram, I have employed a local couple to do all the cleaning and gardening.'

Cassie sat like a stone. Housekeeper. . . staff. . .entertain. . .

It suddenly hit her what marriage to this man would entail. She had not even considered his position—that as a successful businessman Dan would lead a full social life. His wife would be expected to play the role of hostess. The prospect was daunting. And rather ironic, with Cassie dressed as she was today. It brought home the folly of going ahead with the idea.

She lifted panicky eyes. 'Dan, I. . . Are you absolutely sure you want this. . .this marriage?'

His face tightened. 'I thought that that matter was settled,' he stated in clipped tones.

'Yes. . .well. . .I mean. . .'

Cassie's stomach was tied up in knots. So, it seemed, was her tongue. She scooped in a calming breath and tried again. 'Look, Dan,' she said in a conciliatory tone, 'I've been thinking. It's still too soon to tell Jason you're his father. Give him a little more time to get to know you. . .'

He slanted her a sharp look. 'Bargaining time again, is it? I thought everything was settled last night, Cassie. You agreed to marry me.'

'But, Dan, I. . .I hadn't realised what was entailed. I mean. . .I'm a vet, a simple, no-nonsense country vet. I'm not used to the high life. Dinner-parties and such aren't my style. You must understand that if I married you I would not give up my profession to play a social butterfly.'

'*When* you marry me, my dear,' he corrected. 'Not *if*.' He gave her the oddest look. It was almost warm. 'I don't mind if you work after we're married. Be assured, I bought this place so that I can live a quieter existence. I may have to fly away on business sometimes, and no doubt I'll invite the occasional couple up for the weekend, but other than that I want to be a simple family man. Speaking of which, will you still want to work after you fall pregnant?'

'Pregnant?'

'I want us to have more children, Cassie. You must agree that Jason deserves a brother or a sister. You were the one who said you wanted him to have a normal family life.'

Cassie stared at Dan, an appalling thought catapulting into her brain. If she had not stopped him last night she might have already concevied a baby.

One hand fluttered up to her temple. The blood was pounding horribly in her head. She felt dazed. And ill. It felt like a ghastly replay of the past.

'This is all too fast for me,' she rasped. 'Please, Dan, give me more time.' She lifted beseeching eyes to him.

His face grew cold. 'More time for what? To run away? To thwart me further? You've already deprived me of eight years of my son's life. I have no intention of risking any more.'

'I won't run away,' she assured him desperately. 'But you can't expect me to marry you and have a baby just like that. I have other responsibilities, other obligations.'

'Such as?'

'My mother——'

'Your mother is getting married in less than a

fortnight,' Dan interrupted bluntly. 'To dear
Roger, no less.'

Cassie's mouth fell open.

'Jason is very talkative,' Dan explained drily.
'He told me all about his Gran and your boss.
Since even I don't believe that you would be
double-crossing your mother with a man of nearly
sixty, I can only assume that you lied to me last
night. Why, Cassie? Why did you want me to
think your boss was your lover?'

Cassie looked away from his probing eyes and
said nothing.

'Who are you sleeping with that you have to
have a cover for him? Is he married? Is that it?'

Hurt eyes sliced back to him. 'I've only ever
slept with one married man, Dan McKay, and
that was in ignorance. I don't happen to have a
lover. . .at the moment,' she added when she saw
a triumphant light flash into Dan's eyes.

He totally ignored her last words. 'So. . . You
weren't on your way to a romantic rendezvous last
night. Then the red dress was for me, after all,
wasn't it?'

Cassie panicked at the smug way Dan was
looking at her. 'Of course.' Her sarcastic tone
brought a wariness to his eyes. 'But don't flatter
yourself. I came down to Strath-haven last night
planning to seduce you.'

'You *what*?'

'You heard me. I was going to use your. . .your

lust for me to get you to do what I wanted. But I couldn't go through with it. Even with my son's happiness at stake, I couldn't sink as low as that!'

Silence descended on the pair of them. As the fires of temper cooled Cassie began to regret her nasty words. What was to be gained by these continual slanging matches? It was better that she try to bring some civility at least into their relationship.

She sighed. 'I'm sorry, Dan. I. . .I shouldn't have said that.'

'Why not. . .? If it's true.' His voice was bitter.

She gave him a truly apologetic look. 'If you insist on going through with this marriage, then I think we should try to be friends. How can Jason be happy with parents who are always fighting?'

That undermining warmth crept back into Dan's gaze. 'I don't want to fight with you, Cassie,' he said softly. 'I've never wanted to. . .'

Cassie struggled to stay unaffected. Dan was looking at her as though he almost loved her, and it was hard, so hard not to respond. She reminded herself that he was clever at doing that—projecting something that wasn't real. He simply wanted her co-operation, and he meant to get it one way or another.

'Sign, Cassie,' he urged.

Her gaze dropped to the forms. She felt like she was on a roller-coaster ride, being swept along with no control, no real say. If she signed, she would be signing her life away, putting her future happiness into Dan's hands in more ways than one. She hesitated, her heart pounding, her head whirling.

'*Sign!*'

She glanced up into his stubborn face again, knowing that it was useless to appeal to him. She was trapped, as much by her own dark desires as anything.

She signed.

The biro dropped from nerveless fingers to clatter on to the table.

Dan stood up and began to gather the papers. 'Drink your coffee,' he said in a gentler tone. 'You look pale.'

The cup rattled in the saucer as she picked it up.

The brew was rich and hot, but Cassie scarcely noticed. She drank like a robot, all feeling stunned by the enormity of what she had just done.

'You won't regret it, Cassie,' he reassured her.

She stared up at him, long and hard. She saw an incredibly handsome man with striking dark eyes and a sensual face; a powerfully built man, with broad shoulders, a flat stomach and long, athletic legs.

She saw a stranger.

CHAPTER NINE

'DARLING, you look lovely!'

Cassie gave her mother a stiff smile before returning to glance in her dressing-table mirror. She fiddled with her hair for the umpteenth time, poking some escaping tendrils up under the wide picture hat. 'I wish I hadn't let you talk me into wearing white,' she frowned. 'Or this hat!'

'But it suits you! And what's a bride, without a veil or a hat?'

Cassie glared ruefully at her bridal outfit once more. The dress was made of lace, with a fitted bodice, long sleeves and a straight slim skirt, finishing just below the knee. The silk lining was strapless, Cassie's faintly tanned skin showing through the lace on the shoulders and arms. A hint of cleavage was visible on second glance. Despite the colour, the gown did not exude a virginal quality.

Cassie breathed deeply in and out, trying to calm herself. But nothing was going to shift the knots in her stomach. Today was her wedding day. Tonight would be her wedding night. . .

'I can't tell you,' her mother was saying, 'how happy I am about this marriage. It's like a miracle.

Roger and I can live here on the farm instead of moving into his small unit in town, and you and Jason will be just across the bridge. Speaking of Jason. . .I'll never forget the look on that boy's face when Dan told him he was his father. Never! It brought tears to my eyes. And if you noticed, Dan was not without a tear himself. One has to give credit where credit is due, Cassie. No matter what the man was like nine years ago, he's different now. You couldn't ask for a more loving and devoted father.'

Cassie could not agree more. Dan was there every afternoon, picking Jason up from school, keeping him company till Cassie finished work. Jason came home smelling decidedly doggy, but with tales of fun times and computer games, Dan having bought him a whole computer system to make up for eight missed birthdays and Christmases.

But that was all he had bought Jason, which rather surprised Cassie. She had feared that Dan would lavish gifts on his son, spoiling him rotten in an attempt to win the boy's affection. It seemed that that wasn't necessary. Jason was already besotted, talking about his new dad non-stop.

Cassie had also been surprised by local reaction to her coming marriage. Dan had accompanied her and Jason to the cricket game the day before, and once Jason had announced to all and sundry that this was his dad, who was marrying his mum

the next day, they had been swamped with con-
gratulations. The obvious sincerity of the good
wishes had brought a lump to her throat.

Of course, in public Dan conducted himself like
a loving fiancé, holding her hand and smiling,
even putting an arm around her shoulder occasionally. Cassie had found it hard not to flinch
away from his show of false affection. As it was,
she did hold herself stiff and tense when he
touched her. It was all a strain, and on the rare
occasions when they had found themselves alone,
Dan had been silent and grim. Only once had he
spoken, and that had been to ask her to hold out
her finger so that he could check its size for her
wedding ring.

'Hey, come on, you two,' Roger called through
the doorway. 'The wedding chariot awaits.'

Cassie steeled herself and turned towards him.
'Do I look all right, boss?' she asked, a slight
catch in her voice.

Roger whistled. 'If I wasn't already mad about
the mother I'd give our lad across the river a run
for his money.'

Cassie laughed. When she'd first told Roger
about her coming marriage and the reason behind
it, he had been slightly piqued.

'But why didn't you tell me before?' he'd
chided, then added grumpily, 'It all seems
unnecessarily rushed.'

Somewhere along the line, though, he had been

won over to the idea. Perhaps, Cassie thought with dry amusement, it was after Dan had joined them for dinner on Friday night and told Roger about his planned wine cellar.

Cassie's gaze swept over her mother and Roger, who were both looking at her with expectant faces. While she'd lain in bed the previous night, taut and sleepless, Cassie had determined to go through the ceremony showing not the slightest doubt, even going so far as to feign complete happiness. She didn't want her family to worry about her. But it was going to be tougher than she'd thought.

Still. . .

Her lips pulled back into a wide smile. 'Well, folks? What are we waiting for?'

Roger's white station-wagon looked magnificent. The enamel gleamed with polish, the grey upholstery was freshly shampooed. But Cassie almost cried when she saw the bride doll resting on the bonnet, secured there with traditional ribbons. It seemed to represent all that was sweet and loving in a wedding, all that would be missing from her own.

Jason was already in the car, bouncing up and down on the back seat. 'Come on, Mum. We don't want to be late.'

'Brides are supposed to be late,' his Gran remarked as they all climbed in.

'Why?'

Roger laughed. 'So that when she shows up the poor bridegroom is so relieved that he forgets what a damned fool thing he's just about to do!'

'Roger Nolan!' Joan reprimanded. 'If that's the way you think about it, you can——'

Roger silenced her with a quick kiss before accelerating off.

'Oh, yuk!' Jason squirmed. 'I hope you and Dad aren't going to be mushy like that, Mum.'

Cassie's butterflies churned again, but she managed to give her son a reassuring smile. 'I don't think so, Jason,' she murmured.

'That's good! One of the boys at school said you would be kissing all the time, but I told him you wouldn't. He didn't believe me, but he doesn't know you like I do, does he, Mum?'

Cassie's stomach turned over. Out of the mouths of babes. . .

'When are you going to be back from Sydney, Mum?'

'Friday,' she supplied. 'Don't forget your gran is getting married next Saturday.'

'You mean I've got to wear these horrible clothes again?' Jason wailed.

'I'm afraid so.'

'By the way, Cassie,' Roger joined in. 'I've hired a young chap straight out of university to help while you're gone. He can stay on while I'm away too. I might even keep him on permanently if he works out. The practice is big enough, and who knows what might happen in the near future?'

He gave her a look in the rear-view mirror and Cassie knew exactly what he was thinking. She might get pregnant. Thinking about such matters did little for her strained state. It reminded her that in a matter of hours her marriage to Dan would be consummated. She found the prospect terrifying yet insidiously exciting. Nine years. . . Would it be as she remembered? Would the lack of love make a difference?

'Here we are!' Jason squealed, bringing Cassie back to the present. 'Look, there's Dad coming down the steps. Doesn't he look terrific?'

Yes. . .doesn't he? Cassie thought with a jolt. He was dressed in a dark grey suit and white silk shirt, the red tie and handkerchief providing a startling splash of colour. His hair was slicked back from his face in controlled waves, the style bringing attention to his strong, handsome face. His mouth, however, was set tightly in a clenched jaw. His eyes weren't happy. He appeared tense as he strode stiffly across the driveway to their car.

'Our bridegroom looks jittery,' Roger laughed softly.

'Hush, Roger,' Joan hissed.

Cassie swallowed nervously. Jittery was exactly how she was feling, but she doubted that nerves were the cause of Dan's formidable expression.

Maybe he was beginning to doubt the wisdom of marrying a woman he didn't love. Maybe his egotistical and possibly vengeful wish to have her in his bed was on the wane.

Cassie did not look up at Dan when he opened her door and stretched out his hand. She took it, and as he drew her to his feet she finally lifted her eyes. She was taken aback when he smiled at her. 'You look very beautiful,' came his softly spoken compliment.

For a long moment they stared at each other, silent and still, and Cassie felt an overwhelming rush of emotion. It filled her soul, pierced her heart. It was blinding in its intensity.

I love him, came the awful realisation. I've always loved him.

She shrank from the admission, her blood going cold, her hand pulling away from his.

Dan turned away from her, but not before she saw the renewed tightening of his features.

'Come on, everyone,' he said with perfect control. 'The celebrant is waiting for us in the gazebo. Come, Cassie. . .' He turned back and took her hand without really looking at her and the group moved off.

Somehow Cassie made it through the ceremony. She spoke when she had to speak, smiled when she had to smile, kissed when she had to kiss.

Nothing much registered. She felt numb. All she could think was why. . .why. . .why. . .?

He didn't deserve her love. He'd tried neither to win it nor to earn it. Nine years ago he had taken all she had to offer, then deserted her. Now he had swept back into her life, ridden roughshod over her emotions, then forced her to marry him. Even his love for Jason could not justify his selfishness. Cassie felt crushed by the unfairness of it all. Crushed and close to despair.

'You look tired, darling,' her mother said afterwards as they stood sipping champagne on the veranda. Roger and Dan were talking to one side; Jason was playing with Hugo, despire dire warnings about his new suit; the celebrant had departed in the helicopter.

'What was that, Mum?' Cassie said, her manner distracted.

Joan was frowning at her. 'Everything is all right between you and Dan, isn't it, Cassie?'

Cassie pulled herself together. Her mother deserved better than to be forever weighed down with her grown-up daughter's problems. As a parent she had been wonderfully supportive, even renting out her home for some years to go to Sydney to help mind Jason while Cassie went to university.

'Of course, Mum. Don't go imagining things. I'm just tired. You know what a rush it's been this week, shopping for these clothes, packing and moving things over to Strath-haven, organising things for Jason.'

Joan nodded in agreement. 'Yes. . . You'll be glad of a holiday. Just as well you're not leaving till tomorrow, though. Where will you be staying in Sydney? I might need to ring you.'

'To tell the truth, I don't have any idea where we'll be staying. Dan wants it to be a surprise.' Which was a lie. Cassie and Dan had not communicated on a private level at all during the past week. Except for the ring. She glanced down at the wide gold band, truly aware of it for the first time.

Married, she thought shakily. For better for worse, for richer for poorer. . . She looked around. Well, it was certainly for richer, came the ironic thought.

'I'll give you a call in the morning, Mum,' she said, 'and tell you where we'll be.'

'I think it's time we made tracks, love,' Roger called to Joan. 'You know how short these days are. It'll be dark soon.'

Cassie turned to Roger. 'You won't forget to check on Rosie, will you?' she asked, unable to keep the anxiety from her voice.

Roger came over with a big smile on his face and hugged her. 'Now don't you worry your pretty head about that horse of yours, my dear. I wouldn't miss an excuse to come out and visit your mother, now, would I?'

'Is there some problem with a horse?' Dan asked. 'Cassie?' His face was faintly reproachful.

Cassie stiffened instantly, causing Roger to give her a puzzled look. She made a conscious effort to relax and smile. 'Not really. I'm just an old worry-wart. Like Mum. Come on, you two, off you go. I know you have things to do. Jason! Time to go!'

Her mother became tearful now that the time had come to say goodbye. Even Jason seemed subdued. Cassie bent down and gave him a big hug and a kiss. For once he didn't complain about her being mushy. He hung on tightly. 'You're to be a good boy for Gran,' she said, her voice thick, 'and when Daddy and I get back we'll come and get you.'

'Straight away? You promise?'

'I promise.' He sounded so young, Cassie thought, with a clutch at her heartstrings. She gave him another squeeze, shutting her eyes tight to stop her own tears from spilling over. When she opened them to look over Jason's shoulder, she saw that Dan was watching her. His face was totally unreadable.

'Got a hug for me, too, son?' he asked.

For some unaccountable reason, Jason did not answer. Or turn around. He buried his face in his mother's neck, almost knocking her hat off.

Dan knelt down close. 'I'm not taking your Mummy away for long, Jason,' he reassured him gently. 'We'll ring you every night. And next year we'll all go on holidays together. To anywhere you'd like to go.'

Jason glanced over his shoulder, his eyes brightening through the wet lashes. 'To Disneyland?'

'Disneyland it is!'

Jason threw himself into his father's arms with a tiny sob. Tears trickled down Cassie's cheeks, making her turn away.

By the time the small group departed Cassie was feeling like a wrung-out dishcloth. She stood, mournfully watching the station-wagon disappear in the distance, her whole body sagging with exhaustion.

'Come, Cassie. . .'

She did not resist when Dan took her elbow.

'It's bedtime for you,' he said as he took her inside the front door.

She stopped and looked up at him. 'Bed?' she repeated shakily.

'Yes.'

A tremor ran through her. Couldn't he even wait till it was decently dark? A lone tear trickled down her cheek, but she had no energy left to fight him. And he had won, hadn't he? She had never really stopped loving him, no matter what he had done, or what he did now.

He led her upstairs like a child, turning her into the first bedroom on the right. Cassie had been in the room the day before, unpacking her meagre things, only half filling the expansive walk-in wardrobe. At the time she had gazed around the large, almost empty room, pretending all the while to be considering what sort of furniture would suit.

But her eyes and mind had been mainly focusing on the king-sized brass bed, her imagination projecting her forward to this moment in time. Her mental fantasy had been filled with desire and passion, hearts pounding and naked flesh burning. Even after she had gone home the thought of Dan finally making love to her had kept her awake most of the night.

Now her eyes were dull. Her mind blank. Her heart heavy.

She stared down at her marriage bed, and all she longed to do was sink into the downy white quilt, to lay her head on the pillows, to escape into the oblivion of sleep. No desire heated her veins. No passion pricked her senses. She felt listless and defeated—a rag doll.

'Here. . . Let me help you.' Dan removed her hat, throwing it on to a nearby chair. Her hair began to tumble down, but she made no move to fix it. She stood woodenly while he moved behind her and undid the hook at her neck. She remained totally unaffected.

The zip presented little problem for Dan's skilful hands, and once the dress was slipped from her shoulders and off her arms it puddled to the floor. He took her hand and stepped her out of it.

Cassie dimly heard him catch his breath. She had been wearing a white strapless bra and half-slip under her dress, the garments chosen for necessity of style rather than eroticism. But both were made of fine silk, and did little to hide her womanly curves.

She was mildly surprised when Dan took her hand and led her over to the side of the bed, making her sit down. But she showed no resistance, going along with whatever he wanted in a numbed, robotic trance.

Yet when he knelt and gently removed one of her shoes her own breath suddenly stuck in her throat. His touch was infinitely light along her ankle, a seductive feather-caress on her flesh. And when he moved to pick up her other foot she actually flinched, her eyes widening.

His head snapped up to stare at her, his gaze frowning and thoughtful before returning to his task.

Cassie pushed clenched fists down into the mattress at her sides, fighting the unexpected sensations his touch was creating inside her. No. . . She didn't want to feel that. . . Not now! If anything, she wanted to hate him for making her love him.

But what had lain dormant, suppressed by

nerves, dulled by weariness, dampened by champagne, was slowly, inexorably stirring into life.

'Lie back,' he ordered, his voice husky.

She swallowed, but did as he asked, tension gripping her insides. When his hands slid up under her slip to peel back her stockings a sliver of intense excitement shot up her spine. Shaken, she levered herself up on one elbow to watch the stockings join the hat in the corner.

When Dan took hold of both her hands and pulled her to her feet she stared up at him, the battle for control still written on her face. His gaze was intent as his right hand came up to push the hair back behind her ear. It lingered on her neck, the thumb rubbing the sensitive skin at the base of her throat in slow circular movements.

For a moment Cassie relaxed, seduced into compliancy by the mesmerising touch. She closed her eyes, the darkness making her even more aware of Dan's hand. It was delicate and sensual. And arousing. Every nerve in Cassie's body started screaming for him to do so much more. She wanted both his hands on her body. She wanted them on her breasts, her stomach, her thighs. She wanted them to search and invade, to bring her to that excruciating edge when——

The shocking wantonness of her thoughts jerked Cassie's head away from his hand. Her eyes flew open in a type of stunned horror.

Dan glared at her, then swore under his breath.

Clearly angry, he turned away to yank down the quilt. 'Get into bed, Cassie,' came the gruff order.

She hesitated, but slowly climbed in, frowning when he pulled the quilt back up around her shoulders. 'But I thought you——'

'Go to sleep, Cassie!' he snapped. 'Even I'm not so much a bastard as to take you when you're dead on your feet. And so clearly unwilling.'

'But, Dan, I——' She stopped. He was already walking from the room. To call after him, to explain that he had misunderstood her reactions, to beg him to come back was impossible. She had some pride left.

She stared after him, willing him to turn around. But he kept on going. And when the door actually shut, Cassie had no option but to accept that her marriage was not to be consummated that night.

She groaned and threw herself into the pillow, disappointment an acute pain in her heart. And while she supposed that Dan's leaving had been considerate and uncharacteristically sensitive, she couldn't get rid of the feeling that, when the moment had finally come, he hadn't wanted her all that much. The Dan of old would not have walked away, *could* not have walked away. But then, the Dan of old had loved her. . .in a fashion.

Sobs welled up inside Cassie till she could no longer hold them back. She cried and she cried. And when at last she fell asleep, clutching the pillow, she wasn't to know that Dan did come back, some time later.

He stood at the side of the bed, staring down at her, his eyes narrowing when he saw the tear-streaks on her cheeks. He dragged in a deep, unsteady breath, then turned, snapping off the light before leaving the room.

CHAPTER TEN

CASSIE woke to semi-darkness, jerking upright in the bed. It was several seconds before she realised where she was. And that she was still alone.

She sank back down on the pillow and let out a trembling sigh, then reached over to switch on the bedside lamp. She glanced at her watch. Ten-past six. She had been asleep for over ten hours!

Her eyes darted to the door which was slightly ajar. Had Dan come back during the night? If so, why hadn't he come to bed? Why had he left her alone when he'd been so adamant all along that he wanted her?

The more Cassie thought about Dan's actions the night before, the more confused she became. Nothing made sense. Unless. . .

Could it be possible that he really did care about her, that his feelings encompassed more than a wish to possess her physically? It would explain his kind consideration in letting her sleep alone.

Or was it that his desire for her had waned now that he had won his objective? Maybe all he'd really wanted was his ring on her finger and Jason under his roof.

Dismay curled in her stomach. Oh, God. . .
What if he never wanted to make love to her?
What if he had tricked her into a ghastly shell of a
marriage? What if. . .?

Cassie groaned. This was ridiculous! She was
letting her mind run away with her. Dan wouldn't
be so cruel, so ruthless! He wouldn't!

Would he?

She threw back the covers and leapt from the
bed, refusing to allow herself to lie there and
wallow in such imaginings. That was all they were,
she berated herself savagely. Silly, stupid, sick
imaginings!

She dragged in a deep breath and determined
to do something. Anything to stop her mind
churning away!

A walk! That was it! She would get dressed and
go for a walk. That should clear her head. She
would go down to the river and watch the sun
rise. She might even wander over and take a last
look at Rosie. It wouldn't take long, and at least
it would eliminate that worry for the rest of the
day.

Ten minutes later Cassie was showered and
dressed in jeans and sloppy Joe. She made the
bed then tiptoed downstairs to the kitchen. There
she quietly got herself a glass of milk and was
about to leave when she spied a notice-board on
the wall near the back door. She hesitated, then

dashed off a quick message, telling Dan where she'd gone.

The sun had already risen by the time she reached the centre of the bridge, splashing a red gold into the grey waters. But it was cold just standing there, so Cassie kept on walking across, her eyes automatically scanning the horse paddocks in the distance. As her gaze swept over Rosie's field, a prickle of fear clutched at her heart. She couldn't see Rosie. Of course, she could be resting in the shed, but. . .

Cassie quickened her step, almost stumbling down the steps on to the far riverbank. She broke into a run, covering the distance along the path to the makeshift stables in record time, launching herself on to the fence surrounding Rosie's paddock. Where *was* she? Cassie's head swivelled this way and that. The paddock looked empty.

Suddenly Cassie saw her, lying prone in the far corner beneath the old fig tree.

Never had Cassie felt such panic. It tore into her belly, churning, painful, blinding. Oh, dear God, she prayed, pulse pounding, tears threatening. Don't let anything happen to my Rosie!

Cassie was through the fence and at the distressed animal's side in a flash.

'There, there, Rosie,' she cried, sinking down into the dirt on trembling knees and stroking the horse's quivering flanks. 'I'm here, old love. I'm here. Everything will be all right.'

But everything was not all right. The foal was not turned right in the birth canal, and Cassie needed all of her skill and patience to rectify the matter. By the time she had, Rosie seemed almost exhausted. The horse was old and tiring quickly. Cassie felt helpless, but she kept the growing panic out of her voice and talked to Rosie in calm, reassuring tones. 'You're doing splendidly, old girl. Have a rest for a while.' Cassie cradled the horse's head in her lap, letting her long, stroking hands and soothing words give the mare a much needed respite.

Another contraction started. Rosie stiffened. Her head jerked up in pain before wearily dropping back. Cassie felt like crying, but she didn't. Yet the effort to stay calm and supportive was tremendous.

Time ticked away and Cassie's worry increased. She wished she had her bag with her. An injection to strengthen the contractions might have helped. But there again, maybe not. Rosie was not young. Cassie resumed praying.

'Come on, old love,' she encouraged verbally. 'You can do it. Now here comes another contraction. Push!'

And to her surprise Rosie responded magnificently. She gave a great heave, then another and another. And out popped a slithering mass, the protective bag peeling back to reveal a healthy, though very messy foal.

'Fantastic!' Cassie praised, tears of relief and
joy finally gushing over. With the pain gone Rosie
was a different horse, scrambling to her feet and
immediately attending to her foal. It had been
many years since the old mare had given birth,
but animals never forgot. Her long motherly
tongue began the tedious task of cleaning and
drying without any hesitation.

Cassie retreated to the fence, climbing through
to wash her hands under the tank tap, then
returning to lean against the railings and watch
Rosie's meticulous work. The mare did not stop
till her baby's coat was dry, after which she began
the even slower job of nudging the foal up on to
unsteady feet. When finally the filly—Cassie had
craned her neck like a rubber man to acquire this
knowledge—made it up on to those spindly long
limbs, Rosie began directing her gently towards
her teat, swinging her rump around every time
her wayward charge headed in the wrong direction. It was a slow, frustrating process, but Rosie
was patient and kept repeating the manoeuvre.
Success was difficult because the foal, being a
fraction premature, was frailer than some and
kept falling over.

Cassie clapped her hands when the filly finally
remained standing long enough to clamp on and
suck. Her chest felt like it would burst with pride.
For this was her triumph as well as Rosie's. She
had single-handedly brought the mare back from

certain death to this miraculous moment. More tears poured from her eyes as another well of emotion spilled over.

'So there you are!'

Cassie swung round to see Dan striding angrily towards her. He ground to a halt beside her, his anger disintegrating into exasperation when he looked into her eyes. 'Oh, God, no,' he muttered, 'not tears again.' His head shook from side to side in utter frustration. His sigh was weary. 'Even I can't cope with this.'

Taken aback, Cassie blinked up at him.

'And I certainly can't cope with any more of those goddamned confused innocent looks!' he exploded. 'You agreed to this marriage, Cassie. Admittedly, I forced your hand, but you know it's for Jason's good. You could at least give it a chance instead of. . . Oh, hell!' He ran an agitated hand through his hair and his eyes mirrored a type of desperation. 'What else could I do?' he cried in anguish.

Cassie was stunned by his tortured outburst, but the implications of the emotional words slowly penetrated. Could this be a ruthless man talking? A man without feeling. . .cold and callous? Impossible!

'Goddamn it, Cassie,' he burst out again, 'I'm not a saint and my patience is fast drawing to an end. I tried to be a considerate husband last night, didn't I? I put your feelings first, though, damn it all, walking away from you was the hardest thing I have ever done.'

Cassie's heart contracted. He *had* wanted her. He had!

'And what happens?' he raged on, grabbing her by the shoulders and shaking her. 'I get up this morning, only to find your bed neatly made and you gone! I've been looking for you for over an hour. . .worrying. . .not knowing. . . And when I find you, you're in tears again. What am I supposed to do, dammit? Or don't you care what I do——?'

'Oh, Dan,' she broke in breathlessly, 'I'm so sorry. . . I. . . Didn't you see my note?'

His hands dropped to his side in surprise. 'Note?'

'I left a message in the kitchen telling you I was walking over to check on Rosie. . . Obviously you didn't see it. And my crying has nothing to do with you or our marriage. I was crying from happiness.'

She grabbed his arm and turned his stiff, resistant body towards the fence. 'See? Rosie's had her foal. A lovely filly. . . That's why I was so long. She was in labour when I arrived and she needed some help. . .'

Cassie pointed to the mare and foal, who were obviously doing well, the filly standing contentedly in her mother's shadow, Rosie continually checking to see if her little miracle was still there.

'See?' Cassie looked up at Dan, her eyes shining with tears. 'See?' she repeated anxiously when he again said nothing.

He looked long and hard at her. 'I see,' he said at last in a thick voice.

A surge of intense relief swamped Cassie. He understood. . . She had reached him.

'Thank God,' she sighed.

Cassie knew now, beyond any shadow of doubt, that she wanted Dan as her husband—on any terms. She loved him to distraction. And now that he'd shown that his consideration had been based on true caring, that he genuinely wanted their marriage to work. . . Well. . . Cassie was prepared to more than meet him half-way.

'So you weren't thinking of leaving me?' he asked, still frowning.

'No!'

His face remained guarded. 'The tears were really for the horse?'

'I swear.'

Gradually the tautness left his features, but he did not smile. His eyes flicked over Rosie's way. 'This horse—Rosie. . . She means a lot to you?'

'Oh, yes.'

'Why is she so special?'

Cassie proceeded to tell him all about Rosie, talking with the enthusiasm of a true animal lover. 'I couldn't let her become dog food, could I?' she finished, flushed with pleasure at Dan's showing interest.

He gave her a slightly sardonic look. 'No. . .of course not. What about all these other horses?' he went on, dry amusement settling on his face. 'Are they refugees as well?'

'Most of them. But Rosie's special. The others I will sell or give away once they're in good condition. Rosie I could never part with.'

They had begun walking along the path as they talked.

'Why don't you move them over to the island?' Dan suggested. 'There's plenty of good pasture.'

'That would be wonderful, but. . .'

'But what?'

'They'd have to have stables, or a barn. It gets pretty nippy up here in the winter. And they like shelter when it rains.'

'Stables it is, then.'

Cassie frowned. 'Good stables run into a lot of money. Perhaps——'

'Cassie!' Dan stopped. He took her by the shoulders and turned her to face him. 'I can afford stables. I can afford anything you want. Anything! All you have to do is ask and I'll buy it for you.'

Cassie's heart squeezed tight as she stared up into his beautiful, serious face. You can't buy me what I want most, Dan, came the destructive thought, but she firmly pushed it aside. He was trying hard to please her. And he did care. Maybe it was just for Jason's sake, but why quibble about that? Everything was looking a lot brighter than it had when she'd woken up that morning.

She smiled. A marriage where only one partner loved would always be a lop-sided compromise. Better that she begin compromising right now. 'I might take you up on that,' she said with feigned lightness.

'Just name it!'

Cassie could see that he wanted to buy her something, *needed* to buy her something. Perhaps it was his way of making up for forcing her into the marriage. But really, she didn't need anything, and had to rack her brains to come up with a suggestion.

'I. . .I could do with some new tyres on my jeep.'

'Tyres?' He grimaced. 'I offer my new bride anything she wants in the world and she says *tyres*!'

Cassie could see that he was really quite pleased.

'Dan,' she murmured, her voice catching in her throat.

'Yes?' Wariness again showed in his eyes.

'Good morning,' she said. And kissed him.

There was no doubting that she shocked him. He jerked back from her lips as though they were coated in poison. 'And what was that for?' he said, after regathering his composure.

'Nothing. I just felt like doing it.'

He lifted a single eyebrow. 'Did you, now?'

'Yes.'

'Impulsive, are you?'

'Sometimes. . .'

He gave her the oddest look, part sensual, part sad. 'You know. . . I've been thinking. . . We don't know each other very well, do we?'

Cassie stiffened, then turned to walk on. Dan moved with her. She hoped his remark wasn't another lead into his telling her about his previous marriage. Perhaps it was irrational, but she still didn't want to know the whys and wherefores of the relationship that had drawn Dan away from her. Maybe at the back of her mind a few questions niggled. Maybe she would like to know what kind of woman Roberta had been, whether she'd been wealthy or beautiful, and how she had died. And maybe in time she would ask. . . But not now! Her sense of compromise did not extend that far as yet.

'We know enough,' she said tautly.

She kept on walking, but she could feel him looking at her. 'That's a matter of opinion,' he said quietly, but the words carried hurt.

Cassie's regret was instant. They had actually been breaking down the barriers between them. Now, with her stupid jealousy, she had sent them back to square one.

'I'll have to ring Roger later,' she went on,

changing the subject in an effort to smooth over the sudden tension. 'He'll need to check on Rosie and the foal while I'm away. I hope nothing goes wrong.' Her eyebrows scrunched up in a burst of new worry. 'Perhaps we could. . .?' She turned sharply towards Dan.

'No, Cassie,' he said firmly, taking her elbow as they began climbing the steps up on to the suspension bridge. 'We can't. We are going to Sydney this afternoon and that's that. Roger will look after the foal. We need time alone together, away from here, away from everyone. We need privacy.'

Privacy. . . A knot formed in Cassie's stomach as she dwelt on that word and all its connotations. Privacy. . . As they crossed the bridge she darted a surreptitious glance down the river to the point, and the studio. Privacy with Dan meant only one thing. . .

Cassie stopped abruptly in the centre of the bridge. 'Dan. . .'

'Yes, Cassie?'

'Do you still paint?' she blurted out.

'No.'

She frowned.

Dan's mouth curved back into an ironic smile. 'I don't mind telling you why not,' he said, answering her unspoken question. 'Truth is, I haven't had much time for painting over the last few years. I've been too busy making money.'

'Oh.'

'You know, you've never even asked me what business I'm in. I could very well be a drug smuggler, for all you know.'

Cassie was taken aback by Dan's remark, more because of her reaction than the comment itself. She instinctively and immediately rejected any possibility of his being a criminal. Dan might be a typically selfish male, he might even have been an unfaithful husband, but he was basically good. Despite what had happened between them, she felt sure that he didn't deliberately set out to hurt people. He did seem to have a conscience. Somewhere. And criminals didn't.

'I wouldn't believe that for a second,' she stated truthfully.

'That's a relief to know.' His voice was dry. 'I thought you'd believe anything of me.'

'Of course I wouldn't.' She turned smiling eyes up to him and took pleasure in his surprise. 'Well? Are you going to tell me what business you're in, or do I have to drag it out of you?'

He laughed, then frowned. 'It's not that easy to explain.'

'See? Now you know why I didn't ask.'

He laughed again. Cassie liked the sound. In fact, she liked this relaxed, smiling Dan a lot. He seemed so different from the man who had callously told her that he didn't give a damn for her feelings. This was more like the warm, loving Dan of nine years ago, a Dan she could live with.

'How about import and export, property development, rental properties and blue-chip stocks?'

She pursed her lips. 'Sounds impressive.'

'And are you?'

'Am I what?'

'Impressed.'

It was her turn to laugh. 'Sorry. Money's not my thing.'

He sighed, but not unhappily so. 'I guessed as much. By the way, why did you ask me about my painting?'

Cassie swallowed and thought quickly. 'I. . .er. . .was just wondering what you intend doing with the studio,' she improvised, nodding down the river. Initially she had wanted to ask him about her portrait. Whether he had finished it or thrown it away. It had been only half-done when he'd left. But once again such a question felt too close to the bone for their fragile relationship. Better to keep the conversation light. She could handle that.

Dan stared down at the studio. Cassie was perturbed to see his features tighten. 'I intend doing nothing!' His tone was brusque.

'Nothing?'

'That's right. It's there and it can stay there. But I don't plan on using it. Come along.' He took Cassie's arm and propelled her forwards.

'Mrs Bertram always cooks breakfast for eight o'clock and there's nothing she hates more than cooking for absent mouths. She'll be having a pink fit.'

Mrs Bertram was doing no such thing. She was a very efficient woman and had everything under control. Cassie and Dan settled down in the morning-room to a delicious breakfast of freshly blended fruit juices, potato cakes and cheese-flavoured scrambled eggs, along with toast and coffee.

'This is simply delicious,' Cassie complimented, and the housekeeper beamed. 'I think I'm going to become very spoilt.'

'You'll have to tell me what Jason likes to eat, Mrs McKay,' the other woman said. 'Perhaps you could make a list and I can get in supplies while you're away.'

Dan looked up from where he'd been sitting, silently forking eggs into his mouth. Cassie was aware that his mood had changed since she'd mentioned the studio, and, while it bothered her underneath, she was determined to ignore it.

'You don't let Jason eat junk food, do you, Cassie?' Dan said. 'I don't agree with children eating rubbish all the time.'

Cassie prickled with resentment at what seemed like Dan interfering before she remembered her resolution. Compromise was the name of the game. 'Jason has always had a healthy, balanced diet, Dan, but the occasional ice-cream and sweet doesn't do any harm, does it, Mrs Bertram?'

'Of course not! Life would be pretty boring without some luxuries.'

A dry smile pulled at Dan's mouth. 'That's what I keep telling my wife. . . Speaking of diet, Mrs B., you won't forget to feed Hugo, will you?'

'Forget to feed that animal?' The housekeeper made a horrified sound. 'If I did I might end up on the menu myself. That dog eats like a lion!'

'Hugo's a lamb,' Dan countered in mock disagreement.

'More like a wolf in sheep's clothing,' Cassie joined in.

Mrs Bertram cackled. 'Oh, I like that one!'

'Are you women ganging up on me already? Watch it, Mrs B.—I could always hire a male housekeeper.'

Mrs Bertram laughed some more. 'I don't think you will, Mr McKay,' she said, glancing back at Cassie as she walked from the room. 'Not with that lovely bride of yours.'

Cassie blushed as Dan's eyes swung on to hers, their black depths engulfing her with a sudden, hot intimacy. 'She might be right there,' he drawled. 'Maybe I should even hire a woman pilot. What do you think?'

'Your bride might object to that,' Cassie retorted without thinking.

'Would she?' Dan murmured, holding her eyes,

probing, as if wondering whether she cared enough to be jealous. . .or possessive.

Mrs Bertram popped her head inside the door. 'Anyone for more coffee?'

They both declined, but the intimate moment was broken.

'I have to make a few business calls after breakfast,' Dan explained once Mrs Bertram had gone. 'I'm sorry to leave you alone, but I don't want to be bothered with anything while we're away. The helicopter will be here around eleven, and we should be at the Regent in time for lunch.'

Cassie's heart skipped a beat. 'The Regent? Is that where we're staying?'

'Yes. . . Didn't I tell you before? Sorry. I've been staying there occasionally since——' He broke off, his jaw clenched down hard, his chest rising and falling in an impatient sigh.

Since. . .? Since when? Cassie worried. What was Dan thinking about to give him that strained look?

He looked up at her, his expression now one of schooled blandness. 'It's a very good hotel. You'll like it, I'm sure.'

Her palms were clammy where they gripped the cutlery. 'What. . .what should I pack? Clothes-wise. . .'

Dan picked up his coffee-cup and drained it. 'What? Oh, yes. . .clothes. . .' Without batting an eyelid he said, 'As little as possible.'

Her blush was instantaneous. Dan frowned, then laughed. But it was not a light laugh. It had a harsh edge. 'Sorry. I wasn't trying to embarrass you. The helicopter has a weight problem when it carries two passengers. Not only that. . .' He hesitated.

'What?'

'I couldn't help noticing when you brought over your clothes that you don't own much in the way of feminine finery. I'll take you shopping this afternoon. I know you don't care for extravagances, but I have a mind to see my wife in designer labels.' He smiled, and again the gesture did not carry much warmth.

Cassie's whole insides tightened. 'If that's what you want. . .'

His black eyes swept over her, and he muttered something under his breath. There was a slight shake of his head as he got to his feet, as if he were annoyed with himself, but when he looked up at her next his smile was quite charming. 'Haven't you got some phone calls to make as well?' he asked. 'I heard you tell your mother you would ring and let her know where we'd be staying. And I suppose you'll want to ring Roger about the horse.'

Cassie nodded.

'Better get a move on, then. It's nearly ten already.'

He turned away from the table and strode from

the room, leaving Cassie to sit alone and worry.
Why had Dan's moods changed so? First when
she'd mentioned the studio, then later, when he'd
been telling her about the Regent.

What had he been going to say about the hotel?
Probably that he'd stayed there on and off since
Roberta died, she decided.

Cassie vividly remembered his pained look, and
the way he'd had to choke off his words. Had he
loved his wife that much?

Cassie blocked out the surge of jealousy and
tried to face facts. What *was* the truth about their
affair all those years ago? Had Dan really been
getting a divorce, or had his marriage just been
going through a bad patch, with his finding comfort in Cassie's arms, only to race back to his wife
as soon as she needed him?

In the light of Dan's new and kinder manner,
Cassie now wanted to know, really know, for it
was impossible to found a marriage on misunder-
standings and lies. Better she know the truth too,
no matter how it hurt.

Had he somehow loved them both, she mused,
but had ultimately chosen the woman he'd felt he
owed the most allegiance to?

Cassie clung to this most hopeful of the possibilities, reassuring herself that, while Dan had
chosen his wife, he had at least tried to let *her*
down as lightly as possible. Under those circumstances, he wouldn't have mentioned his wife in

that letter he'd written. Neither would he have dreamt of Cassie getting pregnant. That had been *her* stupidity!

No. . .to be fair, Dan was not as black a character as she had believed all these years, Cassie now decided generously.

But, given this line of thought, why *had* he been annoyed when she'd mentioned the studio?

Cassie sighed. She was doing it again, going round and round in circles. And all because they had never really talked, never opened up to each other. There had been too much hurt, too much bitterness, on both sides. They had both been at fault, because they had both felt betrayed; she by Dan's abandonment, he by her keeping him in ignorance of Jason.

So, where do you go from here, Cassie? an inner voice challenged.

She stood up, lifted her chin and squared her shoulders.

To Sydney, came the answer.

To the Regent.

And privacy.

CHAPTER ELEVEN

THE trip to Sydney was nerve-racking. At the beginning the pilot, Paul, kept sliding curious glances her way, making Cassie blush. She imagined that he was vividly recalling the scene he had encountered in the library, which did nothing for her composure.

Dan was broodingly silent for the entire flight, which didn't exactly help. He sat there, in his formidable pin-striped suit, thinking about God knew what, and precluding any attempt on Cassie's part for conversation.

On top of that, Cassie was terrified that they might crash. She hadn't realised she would be afraid, having flown a few times before in her university days. But this was so different. Before she had been in a regular-sized plane. The helicopter seemed too small. And too flimsy! Jason would certainly not be allowed to go up in it again!

She was so uptight, she couldn't even appreciate the aerial view of Sydney as they came in to land. Cassie just stared steadfastly forwards, gripping the sides of her seat with knuckle-whitening force. When the helicopter hovered to a halt on the helipad, her attempt to suppress a sob of relief was without success. Dan darted her a sharp look.

He sighed, but from that moment was solicitous and caring of her needs. He helped her alight and led her numbed body across the cement roof, then held her arm all the way down on the lift ride before propelling her through a busy foyer out into a waiting taxi.

Cassie climbed over into the far corner of the back seat, huddling into it like a frightened animal. Dan gave her another of his exasperated looks before putting an arm around her shoulder and firmly pulling her close.

Cassie slanted him a surprised look, but when she met a stubborn glare in return she gave in gracefully and settled into the crook of his arm. It was really a very pleasant and relaxing position, for his body made a warm haven against the surprisingly chilly Sydney air. Cassie had dressed in a green linen jumpsuit and had thought the long-sleeved style a good choice for a mild spring day, but the clouds had gathered over Sydney and a brisk wind was blowing.

Cassie gradually grew aware of much more than Dan's warmth. His taut thigh was pressed against hers, and she could hear his heart beating. It was going faster, she thought, than his outwardly bland appearance warranted, and making her fertile imagination hurtle forward to the moment when they would finally be alone, when he would take her in his arms and make love to her.

Dan's desire for her was the one thing she no longer sought to question in her mind. No matter how he felt in his heart, he did want her. That, she was sure of.

The Regent was all and more than she had thought it would be. No hotel gained such an international reputation lightly. But it was the service afforded Dan that impressed Cassie the most. It was 'Good afternoon, Mr McKay', 'Lovely to see you again, Mr McKay', 'Of course, Mr McKay', every step of the way. When he casually mentioned that he would like a salad lunch served in his suite the meal practically preceded them, wheeled in on an elegant trolley within seconds of their walking into their rooms.

Cassie was speechless for a second at the sheer extravagance of their accommodation. Dan's wealth came home to her with a jolt as her eyes took in the massive bedroom and sitting-room, and the exquisite marble bathroom, not to mention the spectacular view. This must have cost a fortune, she thought dazedly, and wandered over to stand gazing at the water and the Harbour bridge.

'It's even better at night,' Dan said, coming up behind Cassie to place curving hands over her shoulders. She forced herself to relax back against him, but her nerves were at screaming point.

What now? she worried. A chatty lunch, then a long shopping expedition, with her stomach in knots all the while? Oh, God, she couldn't eat a thing, and she no more wanted to go shopping than fly to the moon.

When an involuntary sigh puffed from her lips he turned her to face him. 'You're not tired, are you?'

She looked up into his tense face, and for the first time appreciated that Dan was under strain as well. His emotions were probably as confused as hers, she realised. Perhaps he thought, as he had the previous night, that she was unwilling. Maybe if she. . .

A nervous spasm claimed her insides, but a mad recklessness drove her to slide her arms up around his neck and lift herself up on tiptoe, her lips hovering just beneath his. 'Make love to me, Dan,' she whispered shakily. 'Now. . . Please. . .'

A frown gathered on his handsome face. 'Now?'

Her heart was thudding in her ears. 'Yes,' she whispered.

His face contorted in almost violent rejection as he wrenched her arms down and whirled away, stalking over to the corner of the room. He stood with feet apart, glaring fiercely through the window down at the traffic below, the rigid shoulders and clenched fists telegraphing his inner upheaval.

For her part, Cassie was totally shattered. Had

she been so wrong? 'Don't. . .don't you want to make love to me, Dan?' she managed to choke out, feeling more wretchedly vulnerable than she ever had in her life. She had bared her heart to him, given up her defences. . .

He turned with grinding slowness to face her, his expression bitter. 'You know I do. But not like this. Not to get it over with because. . .' His hands lifted and fell in a helpless, tormented frustration. 'I don't want you as some sort of maternal sacrifice, Cassie. When I take you to bed, I want you to want me—as a woman wants a man.'

The searing need in his voice forced Cassie to answer with her own. 'I do want you, Dan.'

He made a harsh, guttural sound.

'I do!' she insisted vehemently, taking a tentative step towards him as she searched desperately for words to convince him. The truth now— nothing but the truth would bridge this terrible chasm of misunderstanding. 'I. . .I wanted you last night, too. . .'

Disbelief shot into his black gaze. 'You shrank away from me last night, Cassie,' he accused. 'I didn't imagine that. You hated my touching you. God knows, you warned me. . .that you'd despise me for it. . .but. . .'

She came another step closer. 'No! You misunderstood.' Her voice was urgent, frantic. 'Perhaps at first. . . I wanted to hate you because I. . . Oh,

Dan, don't you see? When you kept touching me, in the end I couldn't help myself. I. . .' The words trailed away as she saw his mouth twist with bitter distaste.

'Couldn't help yourself, Cassie? God, you don't leave a man much pride, do you? Telling me that you're so starved of sex that you'd even tolerate a partner you despise in order to gain satisfaction.'

'That's not what I meant!' she cried. With mounting horror, Cassie began to see what she had wrought with her own stupidly proud words that night in the library—her crazed defiance of his accusations—and all because she had wanted him—only him! 'I don't despise you, Dan, I. . .' She stopped, realising suddenly and shockingly that if she said she loved him, he wouldn't believe her.

'You what? Love me?' He gave a brutal little laugh. 'I'm not a dreamer, Cassie. I've had to face too many harsh realities in my life, and one more is that underneath all your brave little gestures you detest me! Don't bother denying it. I've seen it often enough in your eyes.' One hand shot out to clasp her chin. He lifted her face with cruel fingers. 'You have very expressive eyes, Cassie,' he ground out. 'They don't lie. . .'

His own eyes darkened and narrowed, frightening her for a moment. Then suddenly his hand gentled, his expression becoming heart-meltingly tender. 'Lovely eyes,' he murmured thickly.

'Lovely eyes. . . Lovely mouth. . .' His thumb rubbed over her lips. 'Lovely body. . .' His hands grazed down over her breasts.

He shut his eyes and groaned. His anguish tore at her heart, compelling her to comfort him. Quite instinctively she wrapped her arms around his waist, hugging him to her. 'Oh, Dan. . .don't. . . Please, don't. . . You must listen to me——'

'Listen to what now?' he snarled, pulling back from her. 'More lies?'

Cassie gazed up at him.

His eyes were open, and the hardness had returned.

'I don't want to listen any more,' he grated out. 'I'm tired of it all. So tired. . . Perhaps you're right. Perhaps I should stop fighting myself and just take what you keep offering. Maybe all we'll ever have together is this!'

She had no time to say anything before he jerked her back into his arms, bending his mouth to hers, obliterating the light, obliterating the world, obliterating everything but Cassie's awareness of him, his mouth, his arms, every inch of his body. And after a while it didn't seem to matter if he took her in anger. So long as he took her!

With a low moan she gave herself up to the lips that were devouring hers, to the hands that even now were moulding her body to his with such devastating intimacy. His tongue plunged deep in

her mouth again and again till the thudding in her
temples reached a blinding crescendo.

Finally she had to gasp away to catch her
breath.

'No!' he growled, cupping her face with brutal
hands, glowering down at her with those hot,
black pools. 'Don't do that. . . You asked for this,
and you will do it my way. . . Give me your
mouth. . . Breathe my breath if you have to. . .I
want some part of you joined to me while I
undress you. . .'

The erotic power of Dan's words blasted a
searing heat into Cassie's body. Her cheeks
flamed. Her limbs melted.

'Open your mouth, Cassie,' he ordered thickly,
groaning when she offered her parted lips once
more.

She knew that with her silent submission to his
request she had surrendered more to him than her
mouth. More than her body. This was what he
had once vowed he'd wanted. Her very soul! But
she no longer cared. Let him do with her as he
willed.

His hands were on her clothes, undoing the
buttons on her jumpsuit, dragging it across her
shoulders and down her arms, letting it fall to the
floor around her feet. He stepped her out of her
shoes. Yet all the while their mouths were as one.
The blood was pounding in Cassie's head. Her

whole insides were twisted in a knot of yearning.
Every nerve-ending was jangling.

Her heart stopped as she felt his fingers on the
clasp of her bra, and then her breasts were free,
falling unfettered into his hands. She moaned
softly into his mouth as he caressed her. Her legs
began to quiver.

His kiss kept her from sinking floorwards. His
kiss and his hands. Suddenly they weren't gentle
on her flesh, but she didn't mind. She was as wild
with passion as he seemed to be. She wanted him
to be rough with her breasts, to lift the swollen
mounds, to torment them, to feed this mad,
fomenting need inside her. And he did, ravaging
the tender flesh mercilessly, rubbing the sensitive,
aching peaks till she whimpered in her pained
pleasure.

He stopped kissing her, sliding his hot, moist
mouth down the throbbing column of her neck,
all the while murmuring her name. Over and over
he said it. 'Cassie. . . Cassie. . .'

Then abruptly he scooped her up into his arms
and laid her across the bottom corner of the bed,
letting her head drop over the side, her soft hair
falling floorwards from her neck. He took her
arms and pushed them back on either side of her
head, the position lifting her breasts to his quest-
ing lips. Cassie arched upwards, and as he drew
one ripe, aroused nipple into the hot cavern of his
mouth an animal sound husked from her parted

lips. She found herself staring up at the windows, blindly gazing at the upside-down view.

Cassie's head was spinning. The room was spinning. Dazedly she grew aware that Dan had abandoned her flesh, that he was stripping off his clothes. And then he was back, lifting her head gently on to the bed, running his hands lightly down her body, peeling off the last scrap of clothing between them.

'So beautiful,' he murmured.

She was like liquid, her limbs heavy, her body consumed with a strange, drugging heat. She shut her eyes, making herself more aware of Dan's exploratory touch. His hands skimmed over her flesh, grazing her nipples, circling into her navel, then gently dipping between her thighs.

Her legs parted of their own accord, opening her body to his touch. She became languorous in his caresses, murmuring his name. His mouth replaced his hands, kissing her everywhere. More and more she opened to him. More and more.

She gasped when his lips moved intimately against her, but the pleasure was shockingly addictive. Electric jolts shivered along her veins. A mounting tension claimed her insides.

'Don't stop, don't stop,' came her impassioned, shivering words when he suddenly abandoned her.

His laugh had a harsh, triumphant sound to it. But he bent his head once more, repeating the blissful torture, taking her once again to the exciting edge of the abyss. It was ecstasy and agony. Heaven and hell. 'Oh, God!' she cried, her head threshing from side to side as the excruciating, nerve-tingling, irresistible pleasure was snatched from her once more. 'Please. . .oh, please,' she begged, squeezing her eyes tightly shut.

'Look at me, Cassie,' he growled. 'Open your eyes and look at me!'

She moaned and her eyes fluttered open to gaze pleadingly up at him. He was standing at the foot of the bed, his hair dishevelled, his breathing ragged, magnificent and virile in his nakedness.

'Now tell me you want me!' he ground out.

She opened dry lips. 'I want you——'

'I want you, Dan. Say it!'

'I want you, Dan,' she sobbed.

Never had she seen such a look. So triumphant, yet so ghastly. Every muscle in his face was drawn tight, his eyes glittering like those of a madman. He made a hoarse sound, then stepped forward to abruptly slide his hands under her buttocks. She suddenly felt like a dissociated object, stretched out before him on the quilt, he still standing beside the bed.

'Dan. . . No. . . Not like this. . .'

But he ignored her, his face contorted as he plunged into her, groaning as he wrapped her legs tightly around him, then grasped her hips in a vice-like grip. She had no leverage to struggle against him, and in truth she no longer wanted to struggle. Her body had surged with an indescribable sensation at his forceful possession. Nothing, she thought, could be more right than to be joined like this to the man she loved.

A trembling sigh quivered from her lips. Dan's eyes snapped up to hers. They were half shut in their passion, but they were watching her. His hands reached to cup her breasts, and his palms grazed the tips. Her lips parted with a soft moan.

'It has to be like this, Cassie,' he muttered thickly. 'I have to see your face. . . See your pleasure. . . Don't close your eyes, Cassie. Look at me.'

She did. And found it the most unbelievably arousing experience. Black lights danced in his eyes every time she made a sound, and when she moistened dry lips with her tongue she could see the flames of desire leap in his gaze.

'Your body and mine are one now, Cassie,' he rasped as he ground slowly into her. 'This is how it's going to be from now on. No other men. . . You will know only me!'

Cassie knew nothing. All she knew was sensation. Pleasure. And a blindly escalating tension. It was gripping her thighs, her insides, making her muscles tighten around him. She had to move.

'No!' he gasped. 'Keep still!'

She held herself back for as long as she could, trying to be patient. But, inevitably, her control slipped. Her body began to rock, moving with him, urging him on. Her hands gripped on to the quilt at her sides, her fingers tightening and releasing in time with the primitive rhythm. Her breathing quickened further, as did her movements, and finally he could no longer resist her urgings.

Cassie's body convulsed, her lips parting wide in her gasps of uncontrollable pleasure. And while her body was still shuddering in ecstasy Dan climaxed. Then slowly, exhaustedly, his spent body collapsed on top of her.

For several stunned seconds all Cassie was aware of was Dan's weight on her, then gradually, dreamily, the aftermath of their lovemaking took hold. All her limbs flooded with a heavy languor. A blissful peace seeped into her mind. And in this moment of satiation and contentment, her arms slipped around him, her palms sliding over the warm, damp skin on his back. He had denied her this contact, and now she wanted to revel in it. Love ran from her heart down her arms, through to her fingertips. She caressed his skin, stroked and touched him with the intensity of a woman starved of affection. This was Dan, her man, her love. She hugged him close.

When he suddenly began to roll away she cried, 'Don't go!' and clung on.

For a second he hesitated, then he sank back. Her arms crept back around him in a tightly possessive clasp.

'Oh,. Dan,' she choked out. 'My darling, my love. . .'

His body froze above her. Then with a stiff, jerky movement, he withdrew. He spun away and sat on the side of the bed, his shoulders shaking.

'Goddamn you, Cassie,' he hissed. 'Goddamn you!'

Cassie shot upright, stunned by his unexpected desertion, his savage words. 'Dan. . .' Her hand gingerly touched his shoulder. 'What's wrong? What have I said? Done?'

He rounded on her, black eyes flashing, his expression one of disgust. 'Is that all it takes with you, Cassie? One good lay and you love me? Or do you love every man who satisfies you?'

She shrank back from him in horror, but he swept on, his voice full of derision. 'Let's at least have some honesty in this marriage! So the sex is good between us. More than good. Great! Well, I'm not surprised. It always was. But, for pity's sake, I don't need it served up with false platitudes. OK? Keep the my darlings and loves to yourself!'

Cassie's face began to crumple. She couldn't believe this man. . . He was either incredibly stupid, or heartless! For nine years she had bottled up her love for him. Nine years! And here she was at last, dying to give him every last scrap of it, offering her heart as well as her body on a silver platter. And what had he done with it? Thrown it back in her face!

Appalled, she stared into his flushed, arrogant face and fought her tears, fought them for all she was worth. Her earlier intentions of asking him about his marriage, then explaining everything she had said and done since his return, flew out of the window. She got to her feet, making no attempt to hide her nudity. She drew herself up straight and glared down at him, face proud, eyes chilling with enforced steel.

'Very well, Dan,' she said in clipped tones. 'If you'll excuse me, I am going to have a shower. You said something about taking me shopping afterwards? Forget it! I'm not in the mood. How's that for honesty?'

She spun away and marched over to the bathroom door, where she whirled to face him once more. 'And speaking of honesty, I have one more thing to say. You can stop throwing other men up in my face. There have been no other men. None at all. I lied. You were my first and only lover, Dan. *First and only!*'

Forcing her chin up in crumbling defiance, she threw herself into the bathroom, slamming and locking the door behind her. But as she leant, heaving against the door, the silence from the room outside rushed to haunt her. He hadn't come after her, wasn't banging on the door, didn't beg her forgiveness. She bit her lip and stumbled over to the shower, snapping on the water just in time to let the sound of the teeming jets drown out her sobs.

CHAPTER TWELVE

CASSIE stayed in the shower for ages, unwilling in her misery to face Dan once more. But at long last her water-wrinkled skin forced her to turn off the taps and emerge. She dried herself and dragged on one of the towelling bathrobes supplied by the hotel.

This marriage was impossible, she decided bleakly as she ran her fingers through her damp hair. She couldn't bear to live with Dan every day, sleep in his bed every night, having to keep herself in check, never able to tell him that she loved him. And any hope that in time he might come to love her as she did him was sheer fantasy!

A shudder ran through her at the memory of the way he'd turned on her, so soon after they'd been bound together in what she'd imagined, however stupidly, was a loving union. But it had only been sex on Dan's part. A mere indulging of his carnal desires. On a personal level, he was as cold and ruthless as he'd once declared.

Why had she deluded herself into believing differently—that he was capable of true feeling for her? He'd spelled it out clearly enough for her that night in the library. His one desire had been to secure his son in his life. That was the only reason he had married Cassie. Sex with her was merely a coincidental bonus. Nothing else. For some ghastly, perverse reason she still aroused him—as she had nine years before. If he appeared softer and more considerate occasionally it was only because it suited his purpose at the time. No man wanted a difficult wife. Or an unwilling bed-partner. He'd spelled that out as well.

But love? No. . . He didn't want her love. Didn't want it, didn't need it, couldn't accept it.

Cassie could no longer hide from the obvious truth. Dan had only ever loved one woman. And that woman was dead. . .

Desolation crashed through her, draining the blood from her face, making her lean weakly against the bathroom vanity unit. What on earth was she going to do? How could she cope?

She stared at herself in the vanity mirror, at the puffy red eyes, the swollen lips, the pale, ravaged face.

But you have to cope, her reflection told her. There is Jason to think of, your mother, Roger. . . You knew this marriage wouldn't be easy. You can't run away at the first hurdle even if it's a seemingly insurmountable one. You just have to grit your teeth and bear it.

Gathering herself, she moved over to the door and turned the knob. She felt sick at heart as she stepped out into the bedroom, the prospect of facing Dan again making her stomach churn.

The bedroom was empty.

Cassie raced into the adjoining sitting-room. It, too, was empty. Dan had gone.

Panic set in till she took a hold of herself.

So he's stepped out for a while, she reasoned. He'll come back. . .eventually. And when he does I'll smile and tell him I'm sorry, that in future I'll be a good, quiet little girl, that he can make love to me any time he wishes and I'll. . .

With a sob Cassie sank down on to the sofa and buried her face in her hands. But she didn't cry. She refused to. She steadied her breathing, hardened her resolve, and when her eyes finally lifted they were dry. The years of wretched emptiness had schooled her well.

I will survive, Cassie drilled herself. I will lock my love away, as I did before. It will not be easy, but I will do it. I have to!

Steady blue eyes swept the room, landing on the untouched tray.

Eat! her mind ordered.

Cassie ate. But she didn't really taste a thing. Then she dressed, slowly, back into her lime jumpsuit.

Still Dan had not returned. The light was beginning to fade as the sun sank behind the tall city buildings. Cassie firmly squashed any renewed sense of painc and proceeded to the bathroom, making up her face with relative composure, combing her hair into place. Still no Dan. Her watch showed just after five.

The sound of the telephone ringing jarred into the silence. Cassie raced over to snatch up the receiver from the bedside table. 'Yes?'

'Cassie?'

'Roger?' Surprise lifted her voice.

'Yes. . .'

Roger's heavy acknowledgement and subsequent silence sent a shiver of alarm up Cassie's spine.

'Cassie, I. . .' He sighed and again fell silent. Cassie could hear someone sobbing in the background. It was a woman.

'Oh, my God!' she cried. 'Jason. . . Something's happened to Jason!' She cradled the receiver in both hands to stop herself from dropping it.

'Now don't panic, Cassie. He's all right. I mean. . .well, he's still alive. . . Shh, Joan! He. . .er, was hit in the temple with a cricket ball at practice this afternoon. He's at the district hospital and they say it might only be a concussion, but——'

'Is he conscious?' she broke in frantically.

There was a telling silence before Roger said, 'No.'

'Oh, God,' she groaned.

'The resident here's been trying to contact a

Sydney specialist who's the best, but he's in theatre. It appears that there may be some pressure forming inside Jason's brain which will have to be alleviated. He——'

The bedroom door opened and Dan walked in.

'Just. . .just a moment, Roger,' Cassie rasped.

She lifted stricken eyes towards her husband, who froze on the spot. 'Dan, it's. . .it's. . .' Her voice was choked off by the enormous lump in her throat. A strangled sob escaped her lips.

'What is it?' he demanded thickly. 'What's happened?'

'There's been an accident,' she croaked. 'Jason. . .'

For a moment she thought he hadn't heard her. His face went totally blank. Cassie stared at him, only then noticing his oddly dishevelled state.

Suddenly Dan's face sagged. 'Oh, God, no!' he moaned. 'Not Jason. . . Not him, too. . .'

'Cassie? Cassie, are you there?' came the voice down the line.

'Yes, Roger, I'm here.' She glanced worriedly over at Dan, who looked as if he was going to collapse. 'Yes. . .yes, I'm listening. . . What's that?' Her attention was now all on what Roger was telling her. 'Of course I could. Give me the name of this doctor Jason needs, and I'll keep on trying till——'

The phone was swept out of her hands. 'Roger? Dan McKay speaking. What's this about a doctor?

Fill me in, will you?' His voice was astonishingly steady and firm, as was the hand that pushed Cassie's shoulder down till she was sitting on the bed. Only then did she realise how much she was shaking.

'I see. . . Yes. . . I don't need to write it down. I'll remember. . . I'll let you know when we'll be arriving. . . If I don't get him, I'll get someone else. . . What? No. No, of course I don't blame anyone. Accidents happen. . . Yes, I'll be in touch soon.'

He hung up, but was instantly punching out other buttons, making calls, giving orders. Cassie was dazed by the astonishing change in Dan's manner. What kind of man was this she was married to? One moment totally stricken, the next, a powerhouse of decision-making.

Yet she was immensely grateful for his taking charge, only now fully aware of how close to breaking down she was.

'Come, Cassie,' he grabbed her elbow, lifting her forcibly to her feet. 'We have things to do. Quickly. No, leave our luggage. . .'

There was no time for tears, no time for talk, no time to give in to the sickening lump of fear growing inside her. Cassie was whizzed across the city into the emergency section of St Vincent's Hospital, where she stayed in the taxi while Dan literally ran inside. The minutes passed— precious, life-ebbing minutes. She kept thinking

of her little boy lying in a hospital bed, fluid
building up on his brain, building, building till
something burst. . .

She prayed crazy, bribing prayers. Please, God,
if you spare him, I won't ask that Dan ever love
me. Let him hate me if it will make any difference!
I'll do anything. . .anything. . . Only let my son
live!

Suddenly Dan was back, a big, brusque man in
a white coat accompanying him, who looked quite
disgruntled. 'This is highly irregular,' he was mut-
tering. 'Highly irregular. . .'

Dan glared at the doctor, who glared back
before looking over at Cassie's startled, strained
face. Her eyes clung to him, appealingly, desperately. 'Oh, please,' she begged.

His face gentled. 'Right!' he gruffed. 'We're on
our way.'

The two men climbed in, the doctor in front,
Dan beside Cassie. The taxi lurched off, but they
had now caught the peak hour and were often
held up for minutes at a time without moving. No
one spoke. Cassie found the delays and the silence
unnerving. She started to talk, more to herself,
than anyone.

'Strange how things turn out. There I was on
my way to Sydney thinking that I would never let
Jason go up in that helicopter again. I was worried
about it crashing. And what happens? He gets
hurt at cricket. Cricket. . .' She let out a ragged,

trembling sigh. 'You worry and worry, trying to keep them safe, trying to foresee the dangers. But sometimes, no matter how hard you try, no matter what you do, things happen——'

Her head snapped round at the sound Dan made. It was ghastly. Tormented.

'Yes,' he rasped. 'But do they have to keep happening? First——' He stopped, bruising her heart with a brief, haunted look before he wrenched his eyes away. 'And now Jason,' he said raggedly as he stared steadfastly through the side window.

Cassie's heart went out to him. To lose a wife, then to be in fear of losing a son was surely more than any man could bear. Her hand slipped along the margin of seat between them. She picked up his hand and pressed it gently.

Dan's eyes jerked across. He glared first at her, then down at their linked hands.

'He'll be all right,' she whispered soothingly. 'He has to be.'

He looked at her with eyes that were in hell. 'You don't know, or understand, Cassie. But if I lose Jason too. . .' He closed his eyes, his whole body slumping, his hand cold and lifeless within hers.

Cassie's spirits sank to rock-bottom and silent tears began to fall. Dan was right. She didn't know. They might already be too late.

It was half-past seven by the time the two

helicopters reached the Northern Rivers District Hospital. They landed in the car park, the doctor sprinting ahead into the hospital. Dan and Cassie climbed out and walked together in a tense black silence across the bitumen, up the wide steps and into the lighted foyer.

'Cassie!'

She looked up to see her mother and Roger hurrying towards them. 'Cassie, darling, thank God you're here. Jason's holding on, but——' Joan threw her arms around her daughter and burst into tears.

It was a long night. After examining Jason the doctor ordered immediate surgery to relieve the build-up of cranial pressure, and, despite Roger's suggestion they would be better off waiting at home, all four of them remained in the hospital waiting-room into the small hours of the morning. The tension between the group was so high that neither Roger nor Joan seemed to notice Dan's odd behaviour. He made no attempt to be with his new wife as he either paced the floor or sat in grim silence in one of the chairs. He refused all offers of coffee and had visibly aged ten years.

Cassie wanted to go to him, wanted to do something to comfort him. But she too was hurting. She too was afraid. And it all seemed so hopeless. Family crises either brought people together again, or drove a deeper wedge between them. Theirs appeared to be doing the latter.

Everyone snapped to attention when the doctor suddenly appeared in the doorway. He was smiling. 'The danger's over now, Mr and Mrs McKay. Jason will be just fine.'

An audible sigh of relief reverberated through the room.

Someone breathed, 'Thank God!'

Which Cassie did, fervently, before rushing forward to take the doctor's hands. 'However can we thank you, Doctor?' she cried.

'To see you smile like that goes a long way, Mrs McKay.'

'Can we see him now?' she asked.

'If you like. He's back in his room, but he's still asleep from the anaesthetic.' He glanced over Cassie's shoulder at Dan. 'Well, Mr McKay? Is that helicopter of yours all tanked up and ready to go?'

Dan nodded slowly, apparently too full of emotion to speak.

'Then I must run. I have theatre in the morning, and even geniuses like myself need some sleep.' He grinned and left.

Cassie hugged her mother before turning to Roger. 'You must take her home to bed. . . You, too. . . You've both been under a terrible strain, but Jason is all right now. Dan and I will stay with him.'

When they hesitated, she practically pushed the pair of them from the room. Then with a deep, steadying breath she turned to face her husband. This was no time for personal problems. It was a time for rejoicing. Their son was alive!

'Dan?' Quite determinedly she walked over and curled an arm around one of his. 'Shall we go and see Jason?'

Dan looked rigidly down at her, but his eyes didn't seem to register. They seemed to be in some far off place, where he was enduring his own private agony. 'Cassie. . . I want you to know. . .to understand. . . I have to tell you. You *must* listen!'

She raised startled eyes at the vehemence in his voice. He hesitated, his eyes searching hers as though seeking some sort of reassurance, but suddenly a bleakness invaded his face and he shook his head, expelling a shuddering breath. 'What's the use? It won't make any difference. At least we have Jason. . . All right. Let's go and see him.' He grasped her elbow and propelled her from the room.

Cassie allowed herself to be bustled down the corridor, half wishing she could stop and ask Dan what it was that she should know and understand. In the back of her mind she knew that it had something to do with his wife, but how could she think of such things when her mind and heart were full of Jason and his recovery? And, as Dan said, what difference could it make now?

A pretty young nurse was sitting beside Jason's bed in the small, private room. She stood up and smiled when Dan and Cassie came in. 'I'll be outside if you need me,' she said quietly.

Cassie took one look at the tiny white figure in the bed, his head swathed in bandages, and almost burst into tears again. She clung on to Dan's arm.

'He looks so small, so defenceless,' she cried with a tiny sob.

'So lifeless,' Dan murmured. 'Just like. . .'

Dan groaned and tried to twist away from her, but Cassie clutched his arms. It struck her forcibly as she looked up into his contorted face that, if she truly loved Dan and wanted to make her peace with him, she had to face Roberta's ghost.

'Dan. . . What is it? Tell me!'

He shook his head.

'Is it. . .something to do with Roberta?' she persisted. 'Is that it? If it is, then I want to know.'

Again he shook his head. 'No, you don't. You never wanted to know. Not that I blame you. I've done it all wrong. . .grabbing at you. . .grabbing at Jason. I wanted you both. . .so desperately.' Tears glittered into his eyes. 'All these years of——' His mouth clamped tightly shut and he closed his eyes. 'You'd never understand. . .'

'Dan, please. . .give me the chance,' she

pleaded. 'I. . .I didn't want to know about Roberta before because I was jealous. . .and I couldn't bear to hear about the wife you had loved. . .more than me. . .'

He opened eyes that had known a hell which she could not even guess at. 'I didn't love Roberta, Cassie. And there were times when I hated her from the depths of my soul for keeping me tied to her side. But she had no one else. No one. . ,'

'Tell me about it,' Cassie urged, slipping her arms around his waist. She lifted loving, reassuring eyes. 'Tell me everything.'

He stared at her as though he couldn't believe the words he was hearing, or the way she was looking at him. 'It isn't a pretty story, Cassie.'

She swallowed. 'I can take it.'

'Yes, no doubt you can,' he sighed. 'You're remarkably tough.'

Cassie flinched and looked away.

He swung her chin back with a tender fingertip. 'Don't think I meant that unkindly, Cassie. I admire you. I really do. You're strong and independent, and underneath. . .underneath there lies a heart any man would give his life to capture.'

He gazed down into her startled face and gave a sad little shake of his head. 'It was the blackest day of my life when I had to write that letter to you. . .letting you go. . .' He dragged in a deep, trembling breath then led her over to a visitor's chair at the foot of Jason's bed. 'Better sit down,' he explained. 'This could take some time.'

Cassie sank down in the chair in something of a daze, unsure of grasping on to the hope that was surging into her heart. Dared she believe that Dan had really loved her? That he might still? Yet something—possibly the bleakness on his face— warned her to be careful, to keep her vulnerability in check.

Dan wandered over to stare through the window into the night, his words floating across the room in an oddly detached fashion. 'I was twenty-six when I met Roberta, a qualified accountant with a flourishing business and a flair for finance—well on my way to making my first million. But I was lonely. I wanted to get married, start a family of my own. My only sister had moved to Perth when she married, and taken my widowed mother to live with her. I missed them. . .'

Dan turned and began to pace the room. His voice grew more emotional. Strained. 'Roberta was bright and lovely—fun to be with. A little immature, perhaps, but——' He stopped and slanted Cassie a rueful look. 'I was very arrogant in those days, so sure of myself and of making the future work for me. It didn't seem important at the time that I wasn't madly in love. I'd always believed being madly in love to be a passing illusion and not a good basis for marriage.'

He sighed, and resumed pacing. 'The honey-moon didn't last very long. Roberta was only happy when we were either giving parties or going to them, which wasn't my idea of marriage. I pressed her to have a baby, but she wanted to wait a few more years, have more fun before being tied down with children. Our lives seemed empty and meaningless to me, and our relation-ship deteriorated. Eventually she did become pregnant. . .'

Cassie bit her bottom lip to keep from making a sound. She looked up to see Dan grimacing with remembered frustration.

'. . .but only by sheer accident. I practically had to bribe her to have the child, promising to hire a full-time nurse so that she could continue her socialising.'

Dan's mouth softened into a sad smile. 'But it was worth it. Her name was Maree. . . She was such a beautiful little girl. She——' He broke off and cleared his throat. 'She drowned when she was two years old.'

Cassie's heart squeezed tight, a moan of com-passion escaping from her lips. To lose a child. . . Dear heaven! If she had lost Jason tonight. . .

She lifted agonised eyes to Dan, who was staring at his son, as if reassuring himself that Jason was still alive. Yet when Dan saw Cassie looking at him he turned away and walked stiffly back over to the window, his back towards her.

'Roberta was on the phone when it happened,' he went on in a thick voice. 'She had a charity luncheon to attend and was trying to arrange a baby-sitter after Maree's nanny had fallen ill. Maree must have wandered out on to the patio and fallen in the pool. Somehow the gate had been left unlatched. . . Roberta had had a swim that morning. . .'

'Oh, Dan!' Cassie cried. 'How horrible for you.'

Dan spun round and for a split second Cassie saw the horror of his pain. It was a tangible thing, festering on his face like an open wound. 'I've never known such despair,' he said hoarsely. 'Such misery.'

He sucked in a ragged breath. 'Grief nearly drove me mad. I. . .' He shook his head, struggling for composure. 'Roberta, though, seemed strangely unaffected. If anything her social life increased. She was out practically every night, not returning till dawn. I tried ignoring the evidence of her infidelity at first, but in the end I confronted her. She admitted that there'd been other men. Dozens of them. I don't remember being shattered. Just empty. And sad. But I did begin divorce proceedings and then leave.'

Cassie rose unsteadily to her feet. 'And was this when you came to the island?' she asked huskily.

'Yes. . . My work had been affected by the strain I was under. A business partner of mine was a friend of the van Aarks and he arranged for me to stay there for a holiday. He knew I liked somewhere quiet to paint. . .'

He walked towards her then, and looked her straight in the eyes. 'I loved you, Cassie. You have to believe that. And I needed your love quite desperately. It was something I'd never had before—never believed existed—and I was so greedy for it after losing Maree that I couldn't wait until I was entirely free of Roberta. I had to have you. And I meant to marry you.'

He ran an agitated hand through his hair. 'But then the call came through about the accident. Apparently Roberta had been seeing some chap who owned a motorbike. They'd been drinking heavily and went out for a ride. The bike went out of control on a corner and hit a power pole. Roberta's lover was killed. She was a mess, but alive. Her father rang me from the hospital, begging me to come. He was terribly distressed. He was a widower, you see, Roberta his only child. I couldn't refuse. But it was the middle of the night. . .too late to call you. . .'

Dan's sigh carried an ocean of regret. 'I meant to contact you first thing in the morning, but all hell broke loose. When the doctor came with the news that Roberta would be a paraplegic for life, her father collapsed and died. A stroke. . . brought on by shock. Roberta kept asking for him. God, it was ghastly. I didn't know what to tell her, what to do. Whenever I tried to leave the room she became hysterical. I had her crying and doctors pleading with me to keep her calm.'

Dan lifted tormented eyes to Cassie. 'In the end I had to tell her the truth. It seemed kinder than letting her lie there in a torment of worry and doubt. Oh, Cassie. . .no matter what she'd done in the past, no one deserves to have to suffer that much. When she looked up at me from her hospital bed. . .so helpless. . .so distraught. . .so utterly, utterly alone. . .I knew that I couldn't leave her.'

His sigh was filled with pain. 'So I sat down and wrote you that letter—that rotten, soul-destroying letter.' Dan looked down at Cassie, his eyes flooding. 'Forgive me,' he rasped.

She pulled him close. 'Oh, Dan. . .darling. . .'

There was a moment when he resisted her embrace, then his arms swept around her, hugging her even more tightly than she was hugging him.

Tears flooded into Cassie's eyes as she finally accepted the truth of Dan's love, and the awful tragedy that had shaped his life. She could see now why he had acted as he had when he'd found out about Jason. First when he'd discovered his existence, and then today. . . My God! The control the man must have exercised over himself as he'd frantically gone through the motions of trying to save his son's life.

'I. . .I did my best to make life bearable for

her, Cassie,' he murmured brokenly. 'She. . .died peacefully. . . Some type of embolism.'

'Hush, my love. No more.' She looked up at him, her heart overflowing with love and compassion. She laid a gentle, reassuring hand on his cheek. 'You did everything you could do.'

His hand came up to cover hers and he turned his face into the palm, kissing the warm, soft flesh. A shudder ran through him. 'Tell me you still love me,' he rasped. 'For pity's sake, just tell me that.'

Her eyes swam. 'Don't you know, my darling?' she whispered softly. 'I've always loved you. I'll never stop loving you.'

With a groan, he crushed her to him, his hands cradling the back of her head into the warmth of his neck. 'Oh, Cassie. . . Cassie. . . I love you so much. I thought I'd lost you today, really lost you.'

'Never.'

'But I was stupid, hateful, cruel. . . I thought. . .I couldn't believe——'

'Hush. . . Tell me you love me again,' she murmured.

'I love you,' he said.

'Kiss me.'

He did.

'Mum? Dad?'

They spun out of their embrace and raced to

the bed, hand in hand. Both of them had tears streaming down their faces.

Jason frowned with his one exposed eye. 'Oh, yuk,' he pronounced weakly. 'Sammy Johnson was right. You are going to be mushy all the time.'

CHAPTER THIRTEEN

A PALE pre-dawn grey blanketed the island, a fine mist rising from the river. The helicopter came in low over the tree-tops to be landed with considerable expertise barely twenty metres from the front steps of Strath-haven.

'Home,' Cassie whispered.

Dan gave her a squeeze. 'Home,' he repeated, and kissed her lightly on the forehead.

'You'd better get this machine back to Sydney, Paul,' Dan informed the pilot as they alighted. 'Sorry about the long night.'

'That's all right, Mr McKay. Glad to hear that your boy's going to be all right.'

They watched from the veranda as the helicopter took off, disappearing quicky into the distance.

Dan had his arm around Cassie's shoulders, holding her close against him. She felt wonderfully warm and content. She sighed.

'Tired, Mrs McKay?'

'Oddly enough, not in the least.' She smiled up at him. 'Maybe I'm overtired. In a few hours I'll probably crash.'

'Fancy a walk?'

'A walk? Where?'

She saw his eyes drift down the hill towards the studio, and her stomach automatically contracted. A silly reaction, really. He loved her, didn't he? What was she afraid of now?

But the feeling would not pass. It held an insecurity, a fear of finding out some last hidden factor that might even now spoil her happiness. Life had taught her to be wary.

'OK,' she said, bravely keeping any fears to herself.

'You're very quiet,' Dan noted as they approached the small wooden cottage. 'Are you sure you're not tired? We can go back if you are.'

'No, no, I'm fine. A little cold.' She shivered, but more from nerves than the chill of the coming dawn.

He quickly took off his jacket and placed it round her shoulders. 'Better?'

She nodded, but the feeling of foreboding continued. 'Dan. . . Have you any special reason for wanting to come here?' She hoped that she didn't sound as nervous as she felt.

'In a way.'

'Oh?' She looked up at him, but he said nothing, merely smiled an enigmatic smile. Not even the most suspicious person could have found anything ominous in that smile. But still, Cassie's chest tightened.

They stopped before the front door, its white

panels looking much the worse for wear. Dan stretched out his hand towards the door-knob.

'Maybe it's locked,' Cassie suggested, hoping the ridiculous hope that it was.

'It's not,' came his reply, just before his hand connected.

'How do you know?' she practically accused.

He swung a puzzled face around. 'What?' He turned fully to grip her upper arms. 'My God, Cassie, you look sick. What's wrong?'

'I. . .I don't want to go in there,' she cried, her deep concerns bursting into words. 'I don't want anything to happen. . .to spoil things between us.'

His frown dissolved into a look of such tender understanding that Cassie almost burst into tears. 'Oh, Cassie.' He enfolded her into his arms, cradling her head into his chest. 'My poor love. . .so brave. . .so fine. . . Do you think I would ever do anything to hurt you again?'

He drew back, his eyes soothing her. 'There's nothing to worry about in there. Nothing. This is a very special place, a place where all our memories are good.'

'But I thought you hated it,' she choked out.

'Hate it? Now why would you think. . .? Oh, yes, I remember. . . The other morning on the bridge. You silly ninny,' he whispered, wiping her brimming eyes with soft fingertips. 'I couldn't bear to think about the studio then because it represented everything I'd had once but which I

thought I'd never have again. I was certain you'd
never love me, no matter what you said and did. I
thought your turn-around was all for Jason.
Nothing more. The way you looked at me sometimes. . . It was so different from. . .' He hesitated. 'Come inside, I have something to show
you.'

The studio was exactly as she remembered. One
large room with a fireplace at the southern end, in
front of which stretched a deeply piled brown rug
and an old flowered divan. Around the walls stood
a variety of furniture: book-cases, cabinets, a
table and chairs, an ancient refrigerator. A general air of disuse hung over the whole place,
despite its having been recently cleaned.

Dan took her hand, leading her over and settling her on the divan before turning to stride
across the rug towards an old sideboard in the
corner. Cassie watched, puzzled, as he opened
one section, but when he pulled out a rectangular-
shaped object wrapped in a red felt cloth she
knew instantly what it was. . .

Her throat grew dry as he removed the cover
and placed it on the mantelpiece.

He stared at it for a few seconds, then took
several slow steps backwards. Finally he turned,
as though reluctantly, to face her. 'This is how I
remembered you,' he said.

She stood up and walked towards her portrait,
her mind marvelling at Dan's skill, her heart

hating it at the same time. It was too good, too clear, too telling. . .

'I finished it after I left,' he was saying, 'from memory.'

It made Cassie remember, too. And the memory was unexpectedly painful.

Two big blue eyes looked out at her from the canvas. They were the eyes of a girl in love, deeply in love, blindly in love—the eyes of a girl who would ask no questions, expect no answers, who would give and give without any thought of self. A girl such as she could never be again. If Dan was waiting for her to look at him like this, she thought wretchedly, he would wait forever.

He moved to stand beside her. 'I used to get it out occasionally. Mostly when I'd had a drink or two. And I'd gaze at it for hours.' He let out a ragged sigh. 'You had Jason, Cassie. I had this.'

Cassie turned slowly to face Dan, a dreadful empty feeling in the pit of her stomach. Was this what Dan still loved? she agonised. This fantasy? Was this why he'd come back to Strath-haven— to try to bring the portrait to life?

Dan had told her at the hospital, as they'd sat with a sleeping Jason, the circumstances of his return. He'd found out that the island was on the market quite by accident, months after Roberta had died, ages after he'd given up hope of ever seeing Cassie again. Too long had passed, he reasoned, for her not to be married.

But once he'd heard about the island he'd been compelled to find out. He'd made enquiries at the register of marriages, found no record of a marriage, then looked up the electoral roll to see if she was still registered locally. It seemed impossible that she wouldn't be involved with someone else, but still he had bought Strath-haven and come back, hoping.

Hoping for what? Cassie frowned.

'Dan. . . This isn't me. . .I'm not *her* any more.'

His hand reached out to smooth her wrinkled brow. 'Yes, you are. You're still my darling girl. . .' His expression became glazed, as though he was a long way away. Nine years away. . .

Dismay rolled over her heart.

He must have seen her reaction, for suddenly his face cleared to show a spark of anxiety. 'What is it, Cassie? What have I said?' He grabbed her arms, his sudden movement making the jacket slip from her shoulders. Both of them ignored it as it fell to the floor. He stared down at her, his alarm growing with each second.

Her eyes slid inexorably towards the portrait.

'Oh, Cassie,' Dan sighed. 'Don't go thinking things like that. I haven't shown you the painting to make you feel insecure. I merely wanted to explain that when I met you again, and found you so mature and assured, it came as a shock. I guess for me it was as though you had been frozen in time, and it took a while for my thinking to readjust. You'd grown up. Truly grown up. But once I'd got over the shock I found that you appealed to me even more so. You are a woman such as Roberta never was, or ever could be. Strong and brave. Good and kind. But you are still in essence the girl I painted, with the same sweet, generous heart. You can't imagine how I felt tonight when you told me that you loved me, had never stopped loving me. I thought my heart would burst with emotion. All I can say in return is that I'll try to be worthy of your love. And that I will love you till the day I die.'

Tears shimmered into Cassie's eyes, tears of true joy. 'Oh, Dan. . .'

He bent to kiss her lightly. 'Don't cry,' he murmured. 'I can't bear to see you cry.'

'Even with happiness?' she managed to get out.

'Even that.' One finger traced her lips. 'From now on, all I want to see is laughter in your eyes, smiles on your mouth. Except, of course. . .' his expression carried a warm mischief '. . .when I don't want to see your mouth at all.'

His own mouth descended slowly, giving her time to be ready for him, capturing her parted lips in a heady explosion of passion.

Cassie remembered dimly having wondered if sex would be different without love. Yes, she realised dazedly. Yes, it must be. . . For this was the ultimate, this was insurpassable, this was making *love*.

It wasn't just that his touch pleasured her, nor that his mouth matched hers perfectly. There was an inner joy as he kissed her, an almost miraculous blending of the physical and emotional.

He undressed her quickly, yet with infinite tenderness. Each caress, while tinged with impatience, carried the most undeniable respect.

He said nothing, but his silence was loving, an intense showing of his feeling for her. Nothing was too much trouble. He stroked her body, stroked and kissed her till she was a furnace of longing. And when he came to her she was filled with the sweetest bliss, his possession taking her swiftly along the crescendo of sensation till everything burst around her, showing her ecstasy as overwhelming as the man who had created it.

And as she lay in replete contentment on the rug, her arms around Dan, Cassie realised that they had come full circle. This was where it had all begun. This was where Jason had been conceived.

The thought claimed her quite clearly, with a certainty that would not be denied. A child would spring from this union, a brother or a sister for Jason. This was a new beginning, a going forward. There would be no more looking back.

A long time afterwards, Dan lifted himself from her and brought a hand to touch her face. This he did wondrously, gently, as though in awe of his own feelings.

She looked up at him, not knowing that at that moment, with all her defences down, with her body and soul finally at peace, her eyes were exactly the same as those of the girl in the portrait. Clear and trusting and oh, so full of love.

'Will I never get tired of you, my darling girl?' he murmured thickly.

She smiled. And said one word, a word that carried the total message of their love for each other.

'Never.'

**THIS JULY, HARLEQUIN OFFERS YOU
THE PERFECT SUMMER READ!**

**EMMA DARCY
EMMA GOLDRICK
PENNY JORDAN
CAROLE MORTIMER**

From top authors of Harlequin Presents comes
HARLEQUIN SUNSATIONAL, a four-stories-in-one
book with 768 pages of romantic reading.

Written by such prolific Harlequin authors as Emma Darcy,
Emma Goldrick, Penny Jordan and Carole Mortimer,
HARLEQUIN SUNSATIONAL is the perfect summer
companion to take along to the beach, cottage, on your
dream destination or just for reading at home in the warm
sunshine!

Don't miss this unique reading opportunity.

Available wherever Harlequin books are sold.

SUN

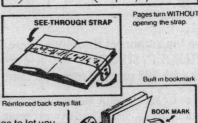

Coming soon
to an easy chair near you.

FIRST CLASS is Harlequin's armchair travel plan for the incurably romantic. You'll visit a different dreamy destination every month from January through December without ever packing a bag. No jet lag, no expensive air fares and *no* lost luggage. Just First Class Harlequin Romance reading, featuring exotic settings from Tasmania to Thailand, from Egypt to Australia, and more.

FIRST CLASS romantic excursions guaranteed! Start your world tour in January. Look for the special **FIRST CLASS** destination on selected Harlequin Romance titles—there's a new one every month.

NEXT DESTINATION:
TURKEY

 Harlequin Books

JTR6

Back by Popular Demand

Janet Dailey

Americana

A romantic tour of America through fifty favorite Harlequin Presents® novels, each set in a different state researched by Janet and her husband, Bill. A journey of a lifetime in one cherished collection.

In June, don't miss the sultry states featured in:

Title # 9 - FLORIDA
Southern Nights
#10 - GEORGIA
Night of the Cotillion

Available wherever
Harlequin books are sold.

JD-JR